PULP
Literature

PULP LITERATURE PRESS
Issue No. 16, Autumn 2017

PULP *Literature*

Pulp Literature Press, Publisher

Jennifer Landels, Managing Editor

Melanie Anastasiou, Acquisitions Editor

Janet Eastwood, Assistant Editor, Acquisitions

Wendy Christensen, Assistant Editor

Daniel Cowper, Poetry Editor

Amanda Bidnall, Copy Editor

Mary Rykov, Proofreader

Kris Sayer, Graphic Designer

Susan Pieters, Consulting Editor

Cover painting, *Seabus*, by Akem. Illustrations for 'The Vanishing Dot' by Rina Piccolo. Illustrations for *Allaigna's Song: Aria* by JM Landels. All other illustrations by Mel Anastasiou.

Pulp Literature: ISSN 2292-2164 (Print), ISSN 2292-2172 (Online), Issue No. 16, Autumn 2017.

Published quarterly by Pulp Literature Press, 8540 Elsmore Road, Richmond BC, Canada V7C 2A1, pulpliterature.com at $15.00 per copy. Annual subscription $50.00 in Canada, $66.00 in continental USA, $82.00 elsewhere. Printed in Victoria BC, Canada by First Choice Books / Victoria Bindery. Copyright © 2017 Pulp Literature Press.

Pulp Literature Press gratefully acknowledges the support of the Canada Council for the Arts.

Canada Council   Conseil des arts
for the Arts   du Canada

Pulp Literature is a proud member of the Magazine Association of BC.

Magazine **BC**
association of

TABLE OF CONTENTS

From the Pulp Lit Pulpit
Autumn Storytelling   7

The River
kc dyer   11

Feature Interview
kc dyer   26

The Magpie Award for Poetry
Oak Morse, Leah Komar, Glenn Pape   29

Stella Ryman and the Ghost at the End of the Bed
Mel Anastasiou   43

Clearing Out Nests
Brandon Crilly   83

Love
Greg Brown   89

The Olde Town Haunt
Patrick Bollivar   97

Think Tank
Susan Pieters   119

The Wind of a Train
Erin Kirsh   131

For Your Convenience
FJ Bergmann   137

The Vanishing Dot
Rina Piccolo   145

Allaigna's Song: Aria
JM Landels   155

FROM THE PULP LIT PULPIT

Autumn Storytelling

It's been a while since we were kids heading off to start a new fall term at school, sometimes in leaf-coloured rain coats. But it's easy to recall the sense of a new start, set against the loss of summer freedoms. It's a true seasonal turning point, not like the warm-to-warmer June solstice. Autumn's changes may influence our storytelling, for the season is rich in colour and transformation. Surprises lurk in shadows, and a ghost may be an ally or a foe.

These days the afternoons pull the winds close around themselves, and lights come on early. We who love reading move to fill the gap between the evening meal and bed with a gripping tale.

How fitting that the story-telling giants often release their thundering sagas and icy

murders in the autumn months. Meanwhile emerging authors, with heroes' determination, stack the pages they worked on through the warmer weather, revise, and find publishers, along with new ideas to set on the cookfire of creative minds.

We wish you all a very happy turning of the leaves.

Jen, Mel, & Sue

With Issue 16, we present you with a new collection of stories selected to delight and entertain you through the misty season. Eat some pie, drink some mead, shiver, and laugh as ...

'The Wind of a Train' by **Erin Kirsh** whistles past in a near future we hope not to see.

Discover the ghoulish side of gentrification in **Brandon Crilly**'s 'Clearing Out Nests.'

Greg Brown's 'Love' offers a chance at a last-minute reunion and a glimpse outside the doorway that awaits us all.

FJ Bergmann's 'For Your Convenience' delivers to Hades, where technology and mythology combine to make a truly punishing afterlife.

Philosophy, family, and the survival of the species unite to take us across the galaxies in 'Think Tank' by **Susan Pieters**.

Patrick Bollivar gives us a ghost story that sends a young woman into a deadly descent with 'The Olde Town Haunt'.

New chapters of *Allaigna's Song: Aria* by **JM Landels** take our heroines deeper into peril with an adventure that will please the most daring hearts and minds.

Judge Renée Saklikar's picks for the Magpie Award for Poetry, from **Oak Morse**, **Leah Komar**, and **Glenn Pape**, show us glimpses of three different types of hell.

In **Mel Anastasiou**'s *Stella Ryman and the Ghost at the End of the Bed*, midnight visitors of uncertain provenance and a mysterious theft at Fairmount Manor propel Mrs Stella Ryman into a new and demanding amateur investigation.

Rina Piccolo's cartoon 'The Vanishing Dot' enchants us with the perspective of memory and the point where everything disappears.

And first off, we invite you to step into feature author **kc dyer**'s haunted world, with 'The River' …

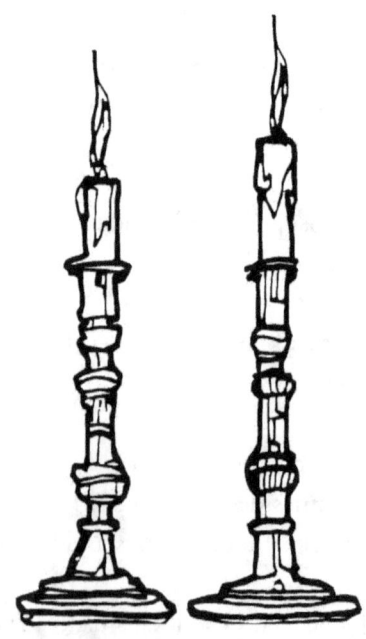

THE RIVER

kc dyer

kc dyer is the author of seven books for teens and adults. Her most recent title, a romantic comedy from Berkley Books, is the internationally best-selling Finding Fraser. Learn more about kc and her books at kcdyer.com.

THE RIVER

I

Lying here on the bank, I can't remember much more than the numbing cold in my fingers and the vile taste of the water swirling through my mouth. I have some recollection of scraping my knees. None at all of falling into the river, or even of what river this is. It's dark and it's cold and I have a wicked kink in my neck, so I can't even turn my head to the right to see where in hell I am.

I have strength enough to turn my head left, so I do it. There are a couple of brown leaves and a discarded page or two of an old newspaper. I can just touch the newspaper with the tips of my fingers — they are too numb to feel anything, but there's enough light to actually see my arm is at least functioning. I stare at the paper — at my fingers on the paper — and I think about pulling it along the ground, sliding it over to cover me. To insulate me from this night and from whatever has put me where I am.

I waken, stiff and damp, with the sheet of newspaper over my face. It slides off with the act of sitting up and I push it indignantly to one side. Has someone covered my face in the night? A few brown leaves are scattered across my legs, too, but that could have just been the wind. I look around, and beside me — not too far away — is a young girl sitting with her arms wrapped around her knees.

"I'm not dead," I say.

She doesn't look shocked.

"I mean — why did you cover my face? I'm obviously not dead."

"I didn't," she says. "Though maybe it's less obvious than you think."

This gives me pause.

The air is warm, and for that I am grateful. My clothes are stiff with mud and still damp from the river water, but sleep has clearly bought me a few degrees of body heat, and my fingers are no longer numb. I flex my hands and the dried mud between my fingers crumbles. I brush it off my jeans.

The girl still sits, still watches. She hasn't moved from her spot. I can see now she's leaning back against a low wall, her back rounded against the stone. Her hands are casually crossed, knees relaxed. She does not look in a hurry to go anywhere.

"What do you mean, less obvious?" I say, at last. My voice sounds more exasperated than I feel, for I am truly curious. I try to soften my tone. "Are you trying to say you thought I *was* dead?"

She shrugs, her shoulders brushing up against the blunt-cut edge of her dark hair. "I didn't think anything," she says. "I pass no judgement either way. I'm just saying it may not have been as obvious as you think. I mean — you were lying there, soaked and muddy, cast up on the bank beside some river. There's a stick in your hair. Judging from that blood stain you've got a decent gash on one of your legs, and you are missing a shoe. It's really no wonder someone put the paper over your face. If someone did."

I straighten my legs out and get a pretty substantial twinge from my left knee. Sure enough, through the tear in my jeans, I can see the skin flapping loosely in a way knee skin usually doesn't.

My stomach does a slow roll.

I swallow. "Well, there's your proof," I say, trying for a bit of black humour. "An arterial leg wound definitely proves I'm not dead."

"Yet."

I shoot her a look, but she doesn't crack a smile.

My right shirt sleeve is hanging by a thread below the elbow, so I tear the torn fabric away and then bind it tightly around my knee, jeans and all.

"That's not going to work," she says. "You need to get it seen to properly."

I double tie the knot right down to the frayed ends of the fabric. She's right, it's not going to hold, but it's all I have.

I shoot another look at the girl. Her position is completely unchanged. She's not moved a muscle to help me, or to get closer, or even to run away. She looks like someone waiting — to watch a parade, or something. No motivation to move. No real anticipation. Just waiting.

Ready.

"Who are you?" I ask.

For the first time, she smiles.

Her face is transformed. She is truly, gloriously beautiful. The tinge of hazel in her brown eyes, the impossibly long dark lashes, the little crinkles that dimple in at the corner of her mouth ...

It's breathtaking to watch.

"Maia," she says. "Who are *you?*"

I push myself to my feet. "My name's Lito," I say. The knee pain kicks in, but after the first surge, it eases back a bit. I take a step to try it out, and everything seems to work the way it's supposed to.

She still hasn't moved from her spot, though she does shade her eyes with one hand to look up at me.

"Well, Maia, maybe you can tell me where I've ended up. I'm gonna need to get some help for my knee here, like maybe a clinic or a local hospital or something. Can you point me in the right direction?"

She shakes her head, smile gone, faced closed down again. "Oh, there's nothing like that around here."

Pretty face or not, I can feel my exasperation beginning to rise. "Okay, fine. Can you at least tell me where *here* is, so I can know which direction to go?"

"You might try off that way, behind the trees. There's a road."

As she lifts her arm to point the way, there is a gentle *pop*. It's really more an absence of sound than anything else. And, just like that, she vanishes.

2

I know, I know. Slow on the uptake.

But really, until the moment the cute, slightly sarcastic girl disappeared, I really hadn't twigged that anything was that wrong.

You know—unfixably wrong.

I mean, obviously, something *is* wrong. A whole mess of somethings.

I am wet.

I am lost.

And I have no recollection of how I came to be here.

When I say she vanished, I don't mean that metaphorically. She is gone. As if she'd never been here before. But not quite. There's still an indent in the grass where she was sitting. I know this because I walk over to it and look for myself. The blades of grass are bent—some are even crushed—in the place where she sat by the low rock wall.

So, yeah. I spend a little time just losing my shit.

I'm not sure how much time, actually.

After a while, I move to right where she was sitting. Feel the ground. Feel the rock wall.

The sun is shining, so I can't tell if there's residual heat from her body left behind or not. I'm on my knees now, running my hands along the ground where she sat. The grass is still crushed, though it springs up under my hands. I find myself patting it back down.

shewashere . . . shewashere . . . shewasreallyhere

Not sure how long this goes on, to tell you the truth. But at some point, I kneel on a rock, and that brings me back to reality in a damned hurry.

My knee is a mess. But weirdly enough, the torn bit of my shirt sleeve is still knotted around my leg, in spite of all the crawling around.

I decide to try manning up, since the snivelling isn't really doing anything for me. I take a final look around the spot where the girl who called herself Maia was planted, just to make sure I haven't missed a dropped hair clip or something.

Not sure why I need tangible proof of her existence.

Not sure who I'll show it to, even if I find it.

But anyway, there's nothing.

The sky is clear — sun's not quite overhead yet. For such a woodsy place, there is no birdsong. With Maia gone and the sound of my own gibbering finally stilled, I am overwhelmed by the quiet of the place. I mean, the leaves rustle. And the river is babbling away, running behind me.

But beyond that?

Nothing.

I take a last look at the low rock wall. She's gone, like she'd never been there. But something of her remains, if only in my mind's eye.

I head for the road she told me about: the road behind the trees.

And on the road?

I meet Bartok.

The road is a mix of gravel and clay, rutted and not very wide — maybe six feet. In places, ruts dig deep into the ground, and grass grows between the tracks.

I walk towards the sun, staring mostly straight down.

After a few minutes, there is clear evidence of asphalt. Crumbled at the edges, weeds growing through in places, but definitely once-pavement. The surface under the asphalt is partly cobbled. Still mostly gravel and clay.

My obsession with the varied road materials means that when I run into Bartok, I do it literally. I think he may have tried to dodge the collision at the last minute, but our shoulders definitely rebound.

I apologize automatically. He is not smiling, but doesn't look surprised at our slightly ballistic first encounter. I look into his eyes, relief washing through me in a tangible wave.

Another person.

I reach out and take his hand.

Shake it warmly.

He doesn't really shake back. We stare at each other in silence a moment.

I have to admit, it throws me that the first person I come across after the rapidly vanishing Maia is a guy in a toga. And, feeling sufficiently thrown off by the surrealism of the moment, I say so.

"A toga," I say. "Really?"

He regards me silently, still, and I know I have been rude. Then I realize in a sudden flood of hopeful shame that he may not understand me.

"I'm sorry," I say, slowly. "I don't mean to offend. I'm lost and need a doctor. Do you speak English?"

My name is Bartok, he replies. You have not been long on this road.

"That's true," I say, equal parts relieved and embarrassed that he has English.

And then to my dismay, I begin to babble. The whole story of the river and the girl pours out of my mouth like vomit. I manage to slam my lips closed just before I get to the bit where Maia vanished.

No need to let all the crazy out at once.

He nods, listening, serious, and then resumes walking. I fall into step beside him. I'm limping a bit, but his pace adjusts to my own.

The river, he says at last. Well, you are certainly not the first. We walk on a moment in silence.

What about the girl? he says. Did she crawl out of the river with you?

"No. She was sitting on the bank. Waiting. When I woke up."

Waiting? For you?

I shake my head. "No — no, I've never met her before."

She vanished! my brain screams. *She talked to me and then she disappeared without a trace.*

But I manage to keep it locked down.

He stops and leans on his staff. Just waiting, he says.

"Yes."

And she is waiting, still, on the river bank?

I swallow down the crazy one last time. "No. I — I don't know where she is now."

He nods, accepting this, and we walk on.

"Mr Bartok, I need to see a doctor. Is this the right way to go to find a clinic or a hospital or something?"

He shrugs — a gentle movement that could be mistaken for the swing of his staff as he walks. Is just Bartok, he remarks. Your limp will improve if you remove that shoe. And it should help lessen the knee pain.

I forgot I'd lost a shoe. Forgot my foot was bare, even when puzzling out the construction of the road.

I stop for a moment and lift up my foot. The shoe is on my right foot, and my injured left knee buckles a bit as I transfer my weight. Bartok holds up an arm to me, and I grab on for balance. I take off my remaining running shoe. Sock, too.

We walk on.

I carry the shoe by the laces, swinging from my right hand. Sock neatly tucked inside.

The road travels on, through the woods. The sun, not quite at its zenith, warms my skin.

No birds sing.

I break.

"She just vanished," I say into the silence. "There was kind of a 'pop', and she was gone."

Ah, he says, and for the first time, he smiles. A happy ending, then.

I stop walking, and Bartok obligingly stops, too.

"Look," I say, and I feel the hysteria bubbling again, just below the surface of my skin. "I just told you she disappeared. How is that a happy ending? How is that anything but completely nuts?"

He looks back the way we came, and my gaze mirrors his own. I see a dotted line following us, tracing our path along the road.

It takes me a moment to realize it is my own blood.

Steady, he says, and reaches out a hand.

His palm twins in front of my eyes and I think briefly about which I should go for. Finally, I close my eyes and just grab.

The world spins a minute and then settles back into place. I feel his hand on mine. His skin is papery, but the strength is there, underneath. His hand slides up under my arm and I think about just sagging into him, just giving way and letting him carry me awhile.

Is not that much blood, he says.

My eyes want to stay closed, my body slumped and leaning.

Certainly survivable, for a time, anyway.

I open my eyes again to see him looking at me kindly. He's essentially holding me with one hand, but there is no sign of strain in his face. Try a deep breath or two, he says, quietly. I find that often helps with shock.

So I breathe and breathe again, and of course I do feel better. Or at least less like fainting.

"I don't know what to do," I say, at last.

The choice is yours as always, he says. The options are never yours to choose, of course. But within those options, the answer rests with you.

He begins to walk again, slowly, and since his hand is still under my arm, I shuffle along beside him. The path underneath our feet now is powdered in a fine, white dust. I decide not to look behind. I don't want another glimpse of the trail I am leaving behind.

I still feel woozy, but the walk is helping somehow. The leaves rustle gently overhead and I can still hear the sound of the river nearby. Suddenly, the brush to one side of the path up ahead is alive with a wild squawking. Twigs and leaves spray across the path.

Bartok pauses, silent.

Two men tumble onto the road in front of us, each trying to throttle the other. They roll around, holding tightly to the other's clothing, screaming and scrambling for purchase.

It's like a cartoon fight — a swirling ball of white dust, with body parts emerging and vanishing: an elbow, the sole of a foot, a glimpse of wildly tangled hair. They are spitting and swearing between punches and head butts. There is a sudden spray of blood across the path, and the fight is over.

The victor stands, one eye swollen shut, across the prostrate figure of the other. He is a compact man, perhaps five and a half feet tall, dressed in what was once a tidy, black suit. His white shirt is torn and blood-spattered, and against all odds, a tidy square of handkerchief still peeps neatly from his breast pocket.

"Asshole had it coming," he says, but he is not looking at Bartok and me. He bends over and reaches out a hand. The other, holding his bleeding nose with a handkerchief he's pulled from his pocket, takes the victor's proffered hand and stands beside him. The man with the bleeding nose is dressed in a suit almost identical to that of his sparring partner, though in navy, not black.

"For Toshiba!" he cries, though it sounds more like *Doshiba*, as his nose is swollen and still bleeding. The two men burst together into identical, delighted peals of laughter, swing their arms around each other's necks, and march back into the bushes.

Behind them, in the middle of the path, remains a carefully polished black shoe.

"What the hell was that?" I say, as Bartok starts to walk again. I stop to peer into the brush where they had broken through onto the path, but all I can see is a tangle of vines and shrubbery. Their voices can be heard, though, like the squabble of chickens, rising and then fading into the distance.

Some cannot cope, says Bartok. Is hard to be lost.

I stop by the man's shoe and stare at it. The familiarity of the image haunts me a few moments, until I realize. I am still carrying my own shoe. By the laces.

"You think he'll be back for it?" I say, but Bartok has moved on.

I look at the shoe again, considering. But it is too small. And the wrong foot.

I hurry along to catch up to the old man, realizing as I do that he is no longer supporting me. I feel a surge of accomplishment.

I can do this.

I fall into step beside Bartok. He walks in the same measured pace. But something is different.

He has gone from looking merely pale to downright translucent.

"Are you — all right?" I ask. He smiles gently and nods. Doesn't slow his pace.

And something clicks.

"Maia," I say. "I get it, now. We're all strangers here. Those Japanese businessmen. You in your toga. Me."

Bartok continues his measured stride, focused on the path ahead. I can see the gnarled wood of the head of the walking stick under his hand.

Through his hand.

"Is she dead?" I ask, pleading now. "Are we all dead?"

I do not have your answers, he says. I only know what I know.

"Well, what is that? What do you know?"

This stops him, at last, and he turns to look at me. The sun is shining straight overhead now, beaming directly down on him. He holds out an arm into the sun, and the light shines through him, angling like a prism to the ground. Near his feet, a tiny rainbow forms.

This so delights him he laughs out loud, but the wind whisks the sound away, tattering into the rustle of the leaves overhead.

What I know, he says, is those who remain here do so until they are forgotten by all they left behind. They follow this endless path by this endless river.

The old man is so transparent now it's hard to hear his words.

"But how long will I be here?" I say. He smiles at me.

Many are lost to the river, he says. Make your cho…

I waken, stiff and damp, with a sheet of newspaper on the ground beside me. The sky is as black as the inside of forever, studded with diamond-chip stars. I can't remember much more than the numbing cold in my fingers and the vile taste of the water swirling through my mouth.

Beside me on the bank I see a shoe.

I reach for it and put it on.

FEATURE INTERVIEW

kc dyer

Pulp Literature: *kc, you began with magic with your YA time travel series Eagle Glen, and have moved to women's fiction with your recent novel, Finding Fraser. Are you happy to continue both genres, and will you continue to expand your work in these genres?*

kc dyer: Absolutely. I have two projects on the go right now. I'm working on Book 2 of a middle grade time-travel epic that will eventually span a millennia; and a contemporary romantic comedy for grown-ups that has just a touch of fantasy for sweetness. But the truth is that I write stories to please myself first, so I figure out all the genre issues afterwards.

PL: *How old were you when you began writing?*

kcd: No idea. Pretty young. But in those days I did more reading than writing. (Gotta get a good foundation, right?) My first journalism gigs were in my twenties, and I remember engaging in aggressive poetry smack-downs with some of the other teachers at my first school. But I didn't earn money for my writing for a long time!

PL: *Is there anybody in particular who encouraged you to start writing novels?*

kcd: No. I did it secretively, unwilling to admit to such a base occupation until I learned if I could manage it or not.

My children knew, and were always encouraging. When I did finally decide to look for help, I joined the CompuServe writers' forum first, I think, and then local writers' groups after that. Amazingly, it took an American writers' forum to inform me about the Surrey International Writers' Conference. When I first heard about it, I thought it was in the UK! I've been to SiWC as a beginning writer, a volunteer, a board member, and a presenter, and I love every part of it. My people.

PL: *Are there books you re-read often?*

kcd: Many, many. I am an inveterate re-reader, usually of the comfort variety. As a kid I read the Anne books dozens of times, and Paddington and Mallory Towers and Gerald Durrell's books. My older cousin gave me her copy of *A Wrinkle In Time*, and I think it may have been my most valued possession ever. These days I read PG Wodehouse, PD James, Kurt Vonnegut, Douglas Adams, Agatha Christie, Daphne DuMaurier, Mary Roach, TH White — so many. I've been re-reading Harry Potter recently (*such* a comfort read!). I'm currently working my way through Iain Banks as a memorial to his memory, listening to Discworld books on Audible, and devouring the Peter Grant series by Ben Aaronovitch. My bedside table is an embarrassing teeter of unread books. I need a new bookcase.

PL: *f you were to stand one book up on your desk today as an inspiration, what would that be?*

kcd: That's too hard a question.

PL: *Who were your character heroes growing up?*

kcd: Harriet the Spy. The kids from the *Mixed Up Files*. Gandalf and Sam and Strider. Anne of Green Gables. The Famous

Five. The Wart. Meg and Charles Wallace.

PL: *What surprised you about the writer's life when you decided to go full time and live the dream of quitting the day job?*

kcd: I'm not sure I'm there yet. Are we ever there? This is a precipitous way to make a living. I often think that interviewers should speak to the children of artists, to learn a few hard truths about 'living the dream'. That said, I know how lucky I am to get to be able to do what I love every single day. I never take it for granted. And I have to say that both my children have grown up doing what they love, too. So maybe some of the dream did ring true!

PL: *Was 'The River' inspired by an image, a feeling, an experience, or something else?*

kcd: No, this story came from somewhere else altogether. A friend told me about a family member, long ago, who went missing from an asylum. That real-life story didn't have a satisfactory ending, so I had fun writing this one, instead.

PL: *What do you love best about living your writer's life?*

kcd: I have been allowed to wander the world, learning things every day and making up stories. It's the perfect job. I love everything about it, and I wouldn't change a thing.

Books by kc dyer

Finding Fraser, 2 0 1 6
Facing Fire, 2 0 1 0
A Walk Through a Window, 2 0 0 9
Ms Zephyr's Notebook, 2 0 0 7
Shades of Red, 2 0 0 5
Secret of Light, 2 0 0 3
Seeds of Time, 2 0 0 2

THE MAGPIE AWARD FOR POETRY

THE MAGPIE AWARD FOR POETRY

The Magpie Award for Poetry saw any number of excellent entries, presenting a delight and a challenge to judges Renée Sarojini Saklikar and Daniel Cowper. Renée Saklikar notes,

The three winners are to be commended for creating work that pleases the senses, exploring a range of issues and keeping an eye and ear on image and rhythm: there's music in here, sure, along with plenty of story. Congratulations to all the poets who submitted work. A pleasure to reach each one. Titles, in my opinion, are mystical things, very hard to get right, and each of the poems selected bears titles that are ineffably correct.

She praises Oak Morse's winning 'Garbage Disposal' for its continuous depth and unity:

Form and the longer line work in tandem to please the eye and ear, both sense and syntax engaged. There is unity of voice, where the third person is taken up with confidence and consistently employed. Enjambment, where the sense of one line folds over and into another, creating opportunity of double-meaning, is a highlight and a measure of why this poem wins first place: it's an incantation, precise and yet metaphorically spacious enough that we can read any number of desires within its precise domestic scenario. Worth re-reading and worth saying aloud.

The first runner-up, Leah Komar's 'Krang', she describes as

Raw, authentic, searing. Unity of voice, in that the speaker of the poem consistently addresses another, 'you', putting the reader in this uncomfortable

and compulsively readable situation. We squirm when we go along with the story. Strong visceral language. Packs a punch and then some.

The second runner-up is Glenn Pape's 'Ghost Town':

Here we have rhyme at the service of both rhythm and longing: the simple line breaks work very well and surprise us with unexpected turns. Precise verbs, precision images, great cadence. This one I'm gonna carry in my pocket.

Congratulations to our winners, and thank you to everyone who submitted and made choosing so difficult, including the other shortlisted poets, Angela Rebrec, Cara Waterfall, Natalie Southworth, Susan Alexander, Troy Turner, and Trudi Benford.

Oak Morse *is a poet, spoken word artist, speaker and teacher who has travelled and toured across the Southeast as a performing artist as well as a teacher of performance poetry. He now is becoming recognized for his recent literary works, which aim to bring attention to a speech disorder known as 'cluttering', which Oak has worked tirelessly to overcome. Oak Morse now speaks and serves as an ambassador for cluttering and writes poetry which seeks to engage readers and immerse them into the cluttering experience. Oak currently lives in Lawrenceville, Georgia, where he works on his poetry collection titled* When the Tongue Goes Bad. *Find more of his work at oakmorse.com.*

GARBAGE DISPOSAL

BY OAK MORSE

we wake up earlier than sparrows to sanitize
the house as if it doesn't already smell like bleach.
we scrub the invisible ring around the tub. we
windex the glass so we can see straight through it.
we make sure the corners are free of cobwebs
and make sure spiders aren't overlooking all this
work we do. we mop right to left, left to right. we
don't open the door for our friends, because we are
on punishment. we've been on punishment for
centuries though.

we ignore the sweat sliding down our backs.
we make sure mama knows that she makes
herself clear. *if y'all don't do it right, you got to do it
over!* mama, mama don't you know you are raising
hell, not young boys? we stop-up the sink so
the water bill won't be higher than jupiter. we
take baths with two inches of water. we scrub
ourselves down to our chromosomes. we brush
our tongues as if that is going to eliminate this
sour taste in our mouths that we have about
mama. we pick up the big stuff off the floor so
it won't tear up the vacuum, or she will tear our
butts up with switches we have to hand-pick
ourselves.

we put elbow grease on the baseboards. we put
pep in our step. we act like we want to keep a roof
over our heads; if we don't, we won't have a roof
over our heads. mama, mama remember you are
raising young boys. we turn off the coffee pot
when we hear it screaming. we slice a hole
in the middle of our fried baloney. we make sure
we only use one thin slice for our sandwich. we
make sure we don't use too much butter because
times are too hard. we warm up leftovers from
ages ago. we grate the cheese as if we are grating
this lifeless life into pieces.

we peel potatoes like they're diamonds, making sure
we don't cut off too much of the essentials. we
remove the rocks from the rest of the dry beans.
we splash a tablespoon of vinegar in almost every
dish. we keep stirring so nothing sticks to the side
of the pot. we put a lid on the pan like we hope
to put a lid on mama's mouth. we try not to let
any grease fly out of the pan, if we do, we use a tiny
bit of detergent to wipe it up. we better not open
that door either because we are still on punishment.

we preheat the oven and imagine one day it will
burn this place down. we clean as we go. we let
the meat marinate long enough. we poke
the centre with a fork to make sure it comes out
clean, all while trying to not let all the heat out the
oven. we make sure the top is golden brown like
it has a tan. we fan off the smoke alarm like we
are trying to fly out of this hell hole. we put our
heart and soul into the casserole. we set the table.
now whose turn is it to bless the food? we better eat
everything that's on our plates. we make our
stomachs into garbage disposals.

we unset the table, we use as little aluminum foil
as possible because it has to last for the next
lifetime. we freeze food hoping it will disappear.
we watch our hands shrivel up like prunes as we
wash all the dishes. we let the pot soak for a little
while, but we make sure we wash it before we go
to bed. we lay our heads down for another early
morning of cooking, cleaning and cursing. mama,
mama don't you know this is not the recipe
for raising young boys?

Leah Komar *grew up in Syracuse and Central Pennsylvania. She attended college in New Orleans and Kyoto, and she has since then lived in Toyama and Austin. More of her writing can be found at thunderandhunger.com. She now lives in Tokyo.*

KRANG

to my mother

You told me I was angry until I believed you.
Words packed in my mouth
like a crowded movie theatre
cut by the scream of a fire alarm
and the sharp accusation of countless lights.

You throw accusations, sharp, after you've run out of plates and
it doesn't matter if I'm seven or lying because
everyone is scrambling and clawing for the exit but
like a nightmare, the door
only opens inward and it's pressed shut
by all of these scared hands
alive and looking for a doorknob.

The bone-cracking truth is I've
always been (looking for and) scared of the way you
take away your hands.
I've laid every stone of my life
around the circle where you
dropped me into existence.

When I find myself running in circles
around my mind,
straight razor in one hand, the past in the other,
I imagine your pelvis cracked like an egg
as I clawed my way out of you.

I must've been a bad movie monster—
claw-handed, yolk and white scrambled violently.
Cronenberg (a word not to use, because you don't know it).
I wonder if it was a relief to be emptied of me
at least until reality was handed back to you (damp-skinned,
    maybe asleep)
As a cloth-faced doctor sewed you back together below the waist,
fingers alive inside of you.

You and I will never talk about the women or men
I've slept with, my fingers alive below other waists, or the way I've
lapped up quiet hours of damp skin and the smell of secret places
like a hungry dog, or the way I
lead out all those words, single file, not panicking,
out of the burning movie theatre and into unsuspecting other bodies,
where, I hope, they will neither grow nor fester.
If they must emerge, broken eggs, clawing hands,

then I hope they at least have the decency to be dead.
Mostly I hope they burn up before they can break any bones
    or ruin any names.
That no one needs to be sewn back together in their wake.

Sometimes I wonder about that doctor who
sewed you up. Such a violent, merciless thing to do.
What did he think about the blood, sticky and warm on his
    hands and
did he pretend not to hear it when you said that I wasn't
who you thought I would be or
if guilt ever weighed on him for what he resigned you to or
for the angry daughter he packed into your life.

Glenn Pape is working on aging gracefully in his old house on a cul-de-sac in Portland, Oregon. Although captivated by reading and writing poetry since childhood, he only began submitting his work upon reaching his mid-fifties. He has been published in The North American Review, The Sun, Poet Lore, *and* The Rhysling Anthology *for science fiction, horror, and fantasy poetry, among other journals.*

Ghost Town

by Glenn Pape

All the stars are silver spurs
the cowboy dreams at night.
And the moon's the hole from an ounce of lead,
right between the eyes.

Night falls hard in the American West.

When the yarn begins unravelling
before it's even spun,
and the hanging tree is waiting,
for the posse to come,

the ghost town rises like a coyote's howl.

I swing down off the saddle
and take a minute to remember what it's like
when boots pound down on solid ground.
The smell of sage blows in from the past.

What are you digging for, you dirt-blind miner?

Is that my mama looking worried
by the window of the general store?
Is that my papa squinting up at the sun?
Let it go.

The legend is always much greater than the truth.

Fact is, a memory is nothing
but an empty shell
next to the cold feel of cocked steel,
or the sweep of warm flesh

against your hungry palm.

That's what we ride for. The ten-gallon hat,
the sweat along the brim, the salt in the sweat
that stings the eyes, the pretty filly's satin haunches—
whatever you can taste or touch or maybe even love a little.

Not the grey fade of what once was. Not these shadows.

When you've never had the guts it takes
to cross the Great Divide,
and a rotgut fifth of whiskey
is the sidekick at your side,

night falls hard in the American West.

Sheriff, I may be getting older,
but I'm not reaching for the sunset quite yet.
You can take my dignity. You can take my pride,
and the rest of the fool's gold

I've got stashed in my saddle.

I've been dancing too long without the clutch
of skin and blood, dancing with whispers,
dancing with footprints painted on the sky.
Sheriff, look me in the eyes.

I'm asking you nice and polite —

leave me something real.
I'd rather feel the fire
from the fangs of a rattler
than be dancing a tumbleweed two-step

with these dim, damned, dusty ghosts.

STELLA RYMAN AND THE GHOST AT THE END OF THE BED

Mel Anastasiou

Mel Anastasiou writes the Hertfordshire Pub Mysteries, the Fairmount Manor Mysteries, and the Monument Studios Mysteries. As well, she is the author of two illustrated 30-day workbooks on story structure, the steampunk-themed The Writer's Boon Companion, and The Writer's Friend and Confidante. For news on published and upcoming new works, visit her website, melanastasiou.wordpress.com.

We present octogenarian sleuth Stella Ryman's newest mystery, The Ghost at the End of the Bed. This is the eighth, or octo, Stella Novella, wherein spectres and thieves walking at midnight force Stella into a tough new investigation.

Stella Ryman and the Ghost at the End of the Bed

Chapter One

Stella Ryman couldn't sleep. She lay on her good Sears mattress, the venetians over her bed shut as tightly as they would go, with her slippy duvet pulled up under her chin. She closed her eyes against the band of pale fluorescent light from Daffodil Corridor, which shone through the night hours in case a resident needed help. But in this, Mrs Stella Ryman, amateur sleuth, was on her own, investigating ways to fall asleep. She had already recited her favourite sleep mnemonic, but *C my name is Cynthia, my husband's name is Chuck* had stopped working for her (although Lucille of the Greek Chorus, to whom Stella had gifted the secret of the mnemonic, said it worked a treat). Stella grew painfully bored but not sleepy. Hours passed. Feeling low on blessings, she decided she might as well count her troubles as if they were sheep. Her daughter Junie, out of touch for months now. Her grandson Derek, so disinterested in life that Stella had never been able to hold much of a conversation with him. Her lack of liberty. The fact that she was down to two true friends: Thelma Hu, perhaps the crankiest blind woman in Canada, and Theo Longbourne, who had the best hair and manners of any male resident at Fairmount but was married to a much younger woman from outside. However, it was worth remembering that her mattress was of exceptional quality, Sears top of the line. Feeling grateful to the salesman who had convinced her to buy it, she fell asleep at last.

Sometime in the night, a ghostly figure woke her when it sat itself down on the end of her bed.

Stella swallowed. She knew who it must be. For, how many ghosts did she know? Just one. *Mad Cassandra Browning.*

"Cassie?"

The figure at the end of the bed didn't answer. Stella peered into the gloom. In the pale light from under the door, she could just about make out the shadowy slender figure perched just beyond the two bumps her feet made under her duvet. But Mad Cassandra Browning—dead now an unknown number of years—couldn't sit still for anything. So Stella decided that the motionless figure was not after all the ghost of Cassandra. It was too slim to be Thelma. It was too short to be Theo, and too silent to be any member of the Greek Chorus except the Nodder, and there was no nodding going on.

Who was it, then?

But no! *Who* was not the question with which to begin. When confronted with metaphysical speculations and ghostly manifestations, one must first examine the geometry of the individual. Stella asked herself two questions.

1. Am I asleep?

2. If so, can I wake up from my dream?

Counting these two possibilities caused her to doze off for

a moment and jerk awake again when the ghost on the end of the bed shifted slightly. Stella blinked, and logic returned with halting steps to her sleepy mind. She realized the fallacy of her earlier attempt at reason. There were never just two lines of logic. She must look for the Third Option. *And keep quite still.*

She reasoned thus:

1. If she were asleep, it didn't matter who was on the end of the bed. This slender person could be anybody her dreaming mind had thought up: Marlene Dietrich, James Dean, a slim being from the outer moons of Jupiter. And it didn't matter, because she would forget all about it before her first sip of tea and bite of toast the following morning.

2. If she was half-asleep, the reasoning was the same.

3. Therefore, the ghost only mattered if she was awake.

Well, then, if she was awake, she decided she must be completely strict with herself and insist that she not see this ghost at all. She could not afford any further doubts regarding her mental status to get about.

Just in time, Stella stopped herself from shivering and so alerting the silent figure at the end of the bed to the fact that she was awake. She then devised a fourth theory:

4. Perhaps the ghostly figure was only a shadow.

She was suddenly sure this was true. Her spirits lifted, and she was just about to sit up in bed when the figure shifted again, and not only did she feel the bed move but she saw the light under the door momentarily darken when the figure's leg moved between Stella and the light.

Damn. She pictured a Fairmount Manor care worker confiding to a new arrival, *See, that's Mrs Stella Ryman. She looks all right, doesn't she, but she's cuckoo. Sees ghosts.*

Well, there was one remaining sure-fire method not to see ghosts. If she didn't want to see them, then she must close her eyes. And once they were shut, she would almost certainly drift back to sleep. She closed her eyes. But as she did, she felt a sudden, unfounded certainty that the figure on the end of the bed was Derek, Junie's boy and Stella's teenaged grandson. And that was ridiculous and illogical, so it had to be a dream, after all (a dream arising out of guilt, no doubt — for avoiding Junie's phone calls and for not sending Derek, over the last few years, a birthday present more personal than a handful of small bills tucked inside a drugstore birthday card). With that uncomfortable thought, she thumped her pillow with her fist and rolled herself up as small as she possibly could with her head under the covers.

In the morning, feeling stale as an old teabag from lack of sleep, Stella dragged herself along, almost not noticing what the cooks Enid and Annie gave them, although she was aware of the crunch of iceberg lettuce at dinner time, always a Fairmount favourite, and caramel pudding of the quick and cheerful kind. She dozed through the afternoon in Corridor Park, the hum of Greek Chorus gossip in one ear and the tap of Thelma Hu's cane in her other, and managed to rest up so well that by bedtime she could already feel the doom-hooded promise of another sleepless night ahead. But she slept at last, and woke once again to see the ghost sitting at the end of her bed.

She lay still, counting people she had known before they died (including Mad Cassandra Browning, although she'd only met Cassie post-mortem). Not surprisingly, since she was eighty-two, this turned out to be about seventy-five percent of people she had known throughout her life personally and professionally, and aside from one school principal who made cow's eyes at her during the free-living 1970s, she couldn't think why any of them would wish to sit on the end of her bed. Counting friends and acquaintances was unsuccessful in the deductive sense, but it did send her back to sleep in the end. When she woke, it was with the dilemma of the elderly: ask for help, get labelled gaga. She took her tan warm-up suit out of her closet and set about getting dressed.

It was all very well saying that you didn't care about what others thought. That attitude was one of the best philosophies to come out of the nineteen sixties — that, and not bothering to wear a hat. But nobody in the whole world wanted to be thought gaga. Everybody wanted to be sane. But what if there were a third option, and something was physically wrong with her?

She whispered, "Go away." The ghost did not.

CHAPTER TWO

Eventually she slept, and woke again feeling so rough that she did a sloppy, unprofessional job of lacing up her shoes. Since the tone for breakfast had not yet sounded, she found her way to Corridor Park, where Iolanthe and Lucille of the Greek Chorus crouched like furies over empty pillowcases upon which they embroidered fruit and vegetables, while Sally the Nodder held ready her scissors to clip the ends of pink and green embroidery floss. Stella moved towards her own chair under the skylight, next to Thelma Hu's empty chair, and nearly tripped over her own badly tied shoelace. She fell back into her seat, hoping that the Greek Chorus, deep in their own crewelwork world, hadn't noticed. She couldn't bear a twitting just now. She was so tired that it was hard to keep from crying. *Emotional incontinence.* Almost as humiliating as the physical sort.

From around the corner just beyond Corridor Park, the light tap of a young woman's step announced the lovely care worker Reliza's approach. A moment later, she had reached Stella's side. Reliza knelt and tied Stella's shoe for her. When Stella thanked her, Reliza looked closely into Stella's face and did something completely unforeseen and out of the ordinary. Reliza sat down in the chair that Thelma Hu usually occupied. The Greek Chorus's needles stopped darting and lay still.

"What's wrong, Mrs Ryman?" Reliza said. "You are not your usual self today."

"I'm having a terrible time sleeping."

"Nightmares?" Reliza asked. "I have those. I'm on a plane, deported to my home, and the plane goes down ... "

"No," Stella said. "I don't exactly have nightmares."

"Do you have cold feet or hands? Or heart palpitations? Or a feeling of panic?"

"Or just odd, busy thoughts? Or twitchy legs?" Iolanthe asked helpfully from the Greek Chorus section of Corridor Park. "Our Stella is always so *busy*."

Lucille, at Iolanthe's side, added, "Or maybe it's gas on the stomach." The Nodder nodded.

"Yes," Stella said.

"Which?"

"All of them." *Plus, I see ghosts,* she might have added, but did not.

"I see." Reliza folded her hands over her middle. She sat silent so long in Thelma's chair that the Greek Chorus returned to their chatter and stitching. Stella grew more and more impatient with this unhelpful, long pause.

"Well, that's what's wrong with *me*," Stella said at last. "What's wrong with you?"

As soon as she'd said it she was sorry. For Reliza didn't answer but covered her face with her hands. Her shoulders trembled, while Stella wriggled herself round in her chair, trying to keep Reliza's troubles, whatever they might be, private from the Greek Chorus.

Whatever her troubles might be. As if Stella didn't know. Reliza and Dr Terry's road to romance was more than rocky.

Stella was a career school librarian and always carried a tissue up her sleeve. She offered it to Reliza. The Greek Chorus, having apparently seen through Stella's attempts to shield the girl, were folding their cloths around their needles and stowing them under their chairs. Like ferryboat passengers who espy a pod of arching dolphins off the port bow, Iolanthe, Lucille, and Sally the Nodder were eager to see new sights.

With fortunate timing, Thelma Hu clattered into Corridor Park. "Who is that sitting in my chair?"

Reliza leapt up to help Thelma into her seat beside Stella.

"Sorry, Miss Hu," Reliza said. "And Mrs Ryman, I'm sorry for crying. I don't mean to be so unprofessional."

Iolanthe, stitching, laughed sympathetically. "A young woman's lot is a hard one."

Lucille added, "Don't feel bad. On your salary, I'd be crying too." The Nodder nodded. Reliza, wiping her eyes with the sleeve of her nylon care worker's tunic, moved off in the direction of the dining room.

Stella glanced from the Greek Chorus to Thelma Hu. She wished that she had better friends than these. *But without social connections, we are just bundles of cells held together by fleece warm-up suits.*

Sotto voce, so that the Greek Chorus might not hear, she said, "Thelma, I have a question for you."

"Shoot," Thelma said.

"Well ... " Stella advised herself to keep it light. "Is I is or is I ain't gaga?"

Thelma snorted. "That is not the question."

"I'd say it's the only question, at Fairmount Manor."

Thelma made a sour face. "How much time do you think people who are not gaga spend wondering whether they are gaga?"

Stella calculated. "None. What *do* they wonder?"

"You should be asking what *I* am wondering."

"What is that?" Stella asked politely.

"I'm wondering, where the hell is my Mah-Jongg box? The one you promised you would search out? With all my fortune in it? It's black lacquer, very shiny and easy to find."

Gah. "Not after ten years," Stella muttered.

"Well, finding it or not is a very good test indeed of whether you are gaga or not, since you want to know so much." Thelma tapped the tip of her cane on the floor.

Stella stood, feeling guilty at not having looked properly for Thelma's heart's desire. What was worse, she was too tired to do a thing about it. "I'm going to find Dr Terry and ask him for a prescription."

From above and around her the tone for breakfast sounded, and slow trickle of humanity filed through Stella's section of corridor towards the promise of tea and white toast. She was sorely tempted to turn about and wash along with them, leaving her visit to Dr Terry for later, or never, depending on the sway of her own mood. *Soldier on, Stella.* She turned left, and right, and left, and eventually she saw the half-open door that resonated with *Dr Terry-ness* to her eye and mind. She came around his door from the blind side and looked in upon him. There he sat. A paperback novel lay open on the desk before him. All around were the rickety shelves he'd put up himself, since he was not an official part of the Director of Fairmount's staff but only a doctor who worked out of a nearby clinic and found much of his work right here in these halls. Dr Terry, who charged your insurance for his optional services but exacted not a dime for his visits to the care home. Dr Terry, a handsome man who was poor at romance but knew his doctoring business. She would tell him of her trouble sleeping. Of the long hours lying awake and all the tactics she had used to banish insomnia and how they no longer worked like they used to.

She might even tell him about her ghosts.

So deeply immersed was he in his book that she had to clear her throat before he looked up. Then she saw that he had not been reading at all. As a career school librarian, who had recommended many a good book to troubled youth, she knew the difference between the eyes of person who has been reading and the eyes of a person who has been crying.

She said to him what she had said to her sorrowful students in her teaching days. "Oh dear, I do hope things are not so bad as that?"

He shook his head between his shoulders, more like a weary old hound than a can-do young doctor. "Oh, Mrs Ryman, I'm sorry. I'm not very wide awake today."

She blinked. "Trouble sleeping?"

"You guessed it. I lie awake for hours, and I don't know what to do about it."

Stella hid her chagrin. "Have you tried mnemonics?"

"I count sheep. What mnemonics do you suggest, Mrs Ryman?"

She taught him the *A, my name is Adelaide, my husband's name is Arnold, we come from Austria, and we sell Appaloosas. B, my name is . . .* "Of course, you must change it round. Wife for husband."

"I'll try it," he said.

She hoped it would work for him as it worked for Lucille. However, this mnemonic and its alphabetic and numerical mnemonical cousins no longer worked for her. So, for this next suggestion, she would have to tread carefully. Very carefully indeed.

She swallowed and took two deep breaths. It took every bit of nerve in her sleep-deprived body to ask the question in a light and subjective manner. "What about . . . sleeping pills?"

Dr Terry looked up. His eyes bored into hers, bright with fatigue. "*Never.*"

"Oh." Stella was so disappointed in his reply that she couldn't help adding, "Then perhaps there's something bothering you and keeping you awake, something in work or in your relationships with friends or family or others that you need to address."

He looked down at his desk, seemed about to answer, and then closed his book with a snap. With perfect courtesy, as if the whole conversation had never happened, he asked, "What can I help you with today, Mrs Ryman? Are you feeling poorly?"

Stella sighed. "No, I'm quite well, thank you."

That night she lay awake, her own words swirling round in her head. *Perhaps there's' something bothering you . . . relationships with* *family . . .* She gazed at her dear old picture on the wall above her bureau and counted the ducks in the pond and the blossoms on the tree above the little farmhouse. *Something in your relationships you need to address.* Stella squeezed her eyes shut. The good Sears mattress was a comfort, but the truth was that she missed her home. A career educator in the public school system, Stella had never been a wealthy woman, but for over eighty years she had done her modest bit for the capitalist society she was part of by acquiring and enjoying worldly goods according to her taste and the modest dimensions of her home. Only four months previously, she had owned a houseful of furnishings and *objets*. Some of them had arrived in her life accidentally, like the black-handled set of free-with-purchase cutlery she had never been able to love; but more of them, for example her Everyman Library collection, shipped to her from overseas, she had husbanded with affection over the decades. And she had sold them all—the treasures of her travels, the carefully-chosen engravings, the good-quality, well-maintained furniture. All gone now. Auctioned off, she supposed, by the agent she had hired. "Sell it all," Stella had told the woman in alligator pumps. "I can't cope. And my room at the care home will be small." The woman had been excited about the engravings, but not the Everyman's books. Thinking over that time, it seemed to Stella that she had left her home for Fairmount Manor as a person flees her burning house, clutching to her breast just a few items that were close to hand: a sackful of nightgowns and fleece two-pieces with coordinating cotton shells; her English countryside replica painting, purchased in Woolworths when she was eleven; and, still trailing its piggy-tail charger, the cell phone Junie had given her the last time she had visited Stella's house.

Soldier on, Stella.

She decided to develop a new Kipling-based sleep inducement method. She reached down behind the bedside table Fairmount provided for her use and switched on the nightlight so that she could study the picture over the dresser. This was the same picture — not a painting, but a picture of a painting — that she had bought from Woolworth's with her birthday money when she turned eleven. Her mother, Tanis Marie Seton, had been against the purchase from the start, suggesting that Stella might get more dollar mileage from a book on good art than a reproduction of bad art. But young Stella hung the picture over her dresser, then as now, and perhaps she more fully enjoyed her purchase independent of the world's approval. Perhaps that was why, over the years, she had kept the faux painting in its faux gilt frame. True, in her home it had done time in a bathroom behind the open door and later cheered the basement wall above the washing machine, but now it was back. And Stella still loved it. So, instead of counting sheep, she counted elements of her picture:

1. the stone farmhouse
2. the pond in the foreground,
3. fully equipped with three ducks
4. the triple-arched waggoner's bridge
5. two cherry trees, limbs thick with pink blossoms against a Gainsborough blue sky

She was still awake, but that was almost to be expected. Now, to get down to brass tacks. She wiggled the nightlight out from the wall and let it fall to the floor, and, like Kipling's young detective Kim, set about recreating the picture in her mind. *Down to the last brushstroke.*

And she fell asleep.

Somewhere in the dark hours of night, she saw the ghost on

the end of the bed, slender, still, and grim. When at last she woke from belated, fitful slumber, her painting was gone.

Chapter Three

In the early morning gloom in her little room, Stella lay on her side, studying the blank spot on the wall over her bureau where her faux Gainsborough picture had rested since her first day at Fairmount. She unclenched her fists and forced herself to deduce an institutional but positive reason her picture might have been taken. For careful dusting? No. To be used in the art lessons offered in the Activities Hall, as an example of the Gainsborough style? She did not believe it for a minute.

Pulling her duvet straight, Stella rose to her feet. She peered behind her bureau to see if the picture had fallen behind it. The space was perfectly empty. Stella dressed in one of her fleece suits, the blue one, and laced up her shoes. She had a good long frowning gander around her room, but nothing else was missing. Just her picture. She brushed her teeth before the bathroom mirror and then, with hard, painful strokes, combed her hair with her pink plastic comb. She held it up and gazed at one side then the other. They were of course identical. "Congratulations, pink comb. I bought you at a dollar store. How long ago?" She remembered the purchase only because she bought so few pink items, preferring in plastics, as in everything else, navy, black or green. "Maybe seven years ago? Does that seem right?"

The pink comb did not confirm or deny.

"I offer these congratulations, pink comb, because now that my picture of the ducks and farmhouse, that I bought with my own money when I was eleven, has been stolen, you are the possession that I have owned for the longest period of time."

She flipped the comb back into her washbag and zipped it up. She stumped back into her bedroom and stood in the middle of the floor. Out of her mouth there emerged a sound that she could not remember ever making before — a growl mixed with a roar of frustration, the sort of noise she had expected from her grandson Derek when he was very young. She ended the noise with a choked-off, ironic laugh and clapped a hand across her mouth.

Her door opened, and a Nameless Dear care worker entered Stella's room. She approached Stella, one hand out in a calming gesture. "Did *you* make that noise, dear?"

"Yes," Stella said, "I did."

"Why on earth would you make a noise like that, dear?"

Because I am old and everything I own is new. "Because I live in a place where staff members enter my room without knocking."

The woman blinked and stepped back. "I'm sure I'm extremely sorry." She turned back as she opened the door to leave. "Don't you think it would be a pretty sorry care home if nobody cared about the residents when they cry out?"

The door clicked shut behind her.

Stella felt suddenly alone in the silence. She wondered whom she wished were there. Not Junie, not Derek. Maybe Sherlock Holmes. He did not solve crimes using fingerprints or police files. He would think it unsporting.

Agatha Christie's Miss Marple spoke up: *You don't need fingerprints or police files, dear. When you have a mind for mystery, you can think things through. Can't you? Use the brain God gave you to figure this thing out.*

Agatha Christie's Miss Jane Marple was right. And the reassurance, though welcome, was also a challenge.

Stella rose to it, and her spirits climbed as she did.

She had already searched her own room, so the question was, ought she to start here in her own Daffodil Corridor and work outwards, or move to the farthest reaches, towards the laundry and effects closet or upstairs into the bright white passageways of Palliative Care? She could easily imagine a thief slipping out through her Room 34 door and glancing round for a hiding place nearby. Here was the door to the unoccupied Room 35, wherefrom Farley Lamoureux and Mrs Alice MacAndrew had lately passed into the realms of possible glory. Stella stepped inside the room.

Room 35 was still furnished with Farley's lawyer's desk, his papers stacked and tucked into plastic shopping bags ready for removal. Those papers had recently been as important to Farley as her missing picture was to Stella. However, since Farley's death at the top of the stairs to Palliative Care, she imagined he'd lost interest in his legal cases, either through non-existence or, more happily, in the busy pleasure greeting long-dead loved ones in Eden. Stella supposed that when she passed from this life, she would lose interest in her picture (unless Eden turned out to have farmhouses, cherry blossoms, pleasantly arranged waterfowl and a true-blue English country sky.) The blinds were up in Farley's room, so that light bathed the room and its furnishings with a possibly misleading innocent empty appearance. Stella used her knees to move Farley's bed out from the wall, searched his washroom cabinet, looked behind his desk, and since it would be ridiculous not to, lowered herself to hands and knees to peer underneath the bed. The space was empty and appeared to have been swept. That gave Stella an idea. Leaving Farley's room, Stella espied Ollie's yellow trolley down at the dead end of Daffodil Corridor by the fire door. She knew he often switched off the alarm there and slipped outside for a smoke. *Fire door. Out for a smoke.* She'd always enjoyed this little — *very* little — play on words, but now she wanted help, not humour. She hurried towards the fire exit and was about to press her body weight on the door lever when it snapped away from her and Ollie re-entered the corridor, looming above her and smelling very much like she remembered school staffrooms smelling in the smokers' paradise in the decades before the nineteen eighties.

Ollie stopped just short of bumping into her. "Stella *ma bella.* Are you all right?"

"Ollie, somebody has taken my old picture, the one you kindly hung up for me, from the wall above my chest of drawers," she said. How do I report a theft?"

"The picture with the ducks? Well, you'd report it to the Director … "

"Mrs Warren." Stella just stopped herself from saying *The Warden.* "Ollie, do you really think she'd care about my picture?"

He frowned. "Or you could report it to a member of staff — that's me. I'll tell Cheryl and Reliza and the others, and we'll all keep an eye out for it. Quite a few things have gone missing. Maybe they're lost."

Maybe not. "Do you happen to know the smallest value the police will interest themselves in?"

"It would have to be worth more than a cardboard duck painting," Ollie said. He added quickly, "*I* like your picture, of course, but why would anybody steal it?"

"Exactly. That picture was valuable to nobody but me."

"I can only think of one reason that anybody might have taken it."

"Say it."

"Well, one of our residents might have seen your picture, and kind of forgotten not to steal it. If so, we'll find it in the end. I'll keep my eyes open, *Stella Portabella*."

With a reassuring squeeze to her arm, Ollie rolled his yellow trolley away along the corridor.

Stella gazed after him. She recognized the validity of his approach to the problem, and she was confident that the other care workers would help her, the way she would have helped a student find a missing pencil or lunchbox when she had been a school librarian. But even as she saw the merit in what he said, she spotted the flaw in his logic. For she didn't think the picture was a thing a dementia patient would take. Jewellery, yes. Food, yes. Paintings that would take two hands to carry, no.

If one accepted that the picture had been stolen not for its (non-existent) value to the thief, nor by a patient with dementia-inspired kleptomania, then it had been stolen because of its vital importance to Stella.

And that meant only one thing. Spite.

And spite could well have destroyed her picture already — ripped it from its frame and shredded the ancient cardboard and paper that had survived everything seventy years of life had brought, only to end up bits of duck and apple blossoms in the bottom of a bin somewhere about the care home.

But perhaps this worst outcome had not happened yet. Perhaps spite was still gazing at the picture, happy and victorious. She must find it and take it back. How to do this without being —she searched for the perfect word, and found it— *rumbled*?

Stella shoved her fists deeply into her pockets. From the little ceiling speaker in the middle of the corridor, the tone for breakfast sounded. In Daffodil Corridor, as throughout Fairmount Manor, residents trickled and then streamed, leaving their empty rooms behind them. Now this was a simple strategy, and one she had employed before: wait until mealtimes and bang through every room on a searching spree. In and out. Surgical. But if Cheryl, Reliza, or Ollie saw that she was not at a meal, they would come to look for her. What with investigating one case after another in this fashion, she had by now missed a great many meals, and had in fact noticed that her fleece warmup suits were hanging a bit loose on her. If care workers came looking for her, worried that she was waning in health, what excuse might she give? She could think of nothing that would not land her in the doctor's office, or the Warden's. Still, her picture was a fragile, elderly item, and so the investigation could not wait.

What she needed was a disguise. Stella's gaze travelled about the room and came to light on the bottom drawer of her bureau, where she kept the books she borrowed from the effects closet. Stella's eyes narrowed. She smiled.

CHAPTER FOUR

Ten minutes later, she was knocking at her first door, that of a woman in Fern Corridor named Dottie. Dottie opened her door and peered up at Stella.

Stella adjusted the books under her arm. "Hello, I'm here to ask you whether you have any books you need returned to the public library." All good detectives in pursuit of a noble goal misrepresented themselves in one way or another. She held up the books, covering the area where the spine labels would go with the fingers of one hand. She walked into the room and looked around.

"This is a very nice room," she told Dottie, although honestly it looked like her own room, without the stolen painting. "The light is good in here."

"What are you looking for?" Dottie's face creased with worry. "I don't have a cat in my room. Not allowed."

"Not at all. I didn't mean to upset you, Dottie, believe me. I'm just here to ask if you have any library books. Not cats."

"Oh, good." Dottie pressed the flat of her hand to her breast. "I'm so relieved."

Stella sighed as she stepped back into the hallway. On the one hand, Miss Marple and Sherlock Holmes didn't have to deal with Fairmount Manor residents. On the other hand, Stella reminded herself that she wasn't in the amateur sleuth game because it was easy.

Stella approached the next door, decoy books tucked under her arm. Her stomach growled, and she wished she might have set out on her quest after lunch, in the manner of explorers waiting for the snows of winter to recede.

Soldier on, Stella. She knocked on the door.

A curly white head showed in the doorway.

Stella said, "Hello there. Do you have any library books to return?"

The curly-headed woman snapped back, "Do you know how to fix a television?"

"No," Stella said. But she realized that her answer was both counterproductive and untrue. "Yes, I do know something about it. I oversaw my school's technology closet for thirty years."

"I'm losing my mind, trying to deal with this set," the woman said. "And I'm missing my show."

The woman stepped back and Stella advanced into the room. She was sorry to see that the television in question appeared to be a recent model. The newer the model, the more incalculable the options for setting its operation to rights. She remembered the first of the new generation of television sets, a 1985 model that had shown nothing but a blue screen and a series of occult numbers in white text, no matter what any teacher or student did to it.

She met the curly-headed woman's gaze and felt a wave of sympathy. This did not, however, stop her from glancing round the room. She worried for a moment about seeing under beds, but the rules for keeping the floor uncluttered for mopping were so stringently kept — even Ollie, normally so cheerful, turned grumpy if you left so much as a sock under there — and the beds so frequently hauled away from the walls that there were very few places inside a resident's bedroom to hide a picture. The only trouble was that there were so very many residents' bedrooms. Time to move on to the next. But first, she brought all her librarian's technological savvy to the problem of the television:

1. Was the set plugged into the wall? Yes.

2. Were all the cords plugged into the back? Yes.

3. What happened when the power switch turned on and off? Nothing.

4. What happened when you pushed every little button along the bottom and side edges?

By gum, a picture appeared on the screen. The curly-headed

woman clasped her hands together. "And it's Channel Three! I haven't had Channel Three for months."

Stella might have left then, but the woman picked up two clickers and began to click in a rhythmical fashion. "I would leave things be if I were you," Stella said. "And watch Channel Three."

The curly-headed woman looked up from the clickers. Her face fell, and she sat down on her bed and turned to watch with the look of a woman who will never get to see her favourite show again. Stella said, "Here. Give me the clickers." She clicked from right to left to right to left, all possible combinations until her thumbs ached and she had forgotten which numbers she began with, and three-digit numbers appeared, mounting ever higher on a black screen. All hope seemed lost. Stella closed her eyes and carried on anyway. At last a roar of delight emanated from the television: an audience's approbation of a bright-faced contestant.

"My show. You've found it." The woman's face gleamed as brightly as the contestant on the screen. With a last glance at the empty floor at the end of the bed, Stella took her leave.

Knock, knock.

The next door opened. A woman Stella was pretty sure was named Harriet said, "Did you bring it?"

Stella had no idea what Harriet was hoping for, but she saw the green light of anticipation in the woman's eye. It was obvious that to ask what *it* was that she was meant to have brought would be cruel. Instead Stella took from under her arm John D MacDonald's *The Long Blue Goodbye*, which she had only half finished reading. With reluctance, for it was a ripping tale, she pressed the paperback between Harriet's slender palms. "You'll love it."

Harriet thanked her and opened the book. With a quick glance about Harriet's room, Stella left her to it.

Knock, knock.

This time the door stayed shut. Stella examined the line of shadow under the door. The shadow moved, and there was a shushing sound of slippers on floor tiles.

With a silent *I'm sorry* for all the negative thoughts she'd had in her life about door-to-door salesmen—the blanket, mute apology did not extend to cold callers on the telephone or the writers of spam emails—Stella knocked again.

A moment's more shuffling ensued. Stella heard the sound of breath caught in somebody's throat. At last the door opened.

Just a crack.

"I'm afraid," an almost inaudible voice from within said, "I can't talk to anybody today."

Stella leaned up close to the cracked door and made out a thin face inside. She smiled reassuringly. "It's all right. You don't have to talk. And I won't say a word."

The woman held open the door for Stella. Stella glanced around her, while the woman sat on her bed, gazing down with her hands folded in front of her like a good prisoner. Stella wanted to say, "Listen, you may feel better tomorrow. The human spirit is very good at overcoming every sort of sorrow and adversity."

But she couldn't break her promise not to speak. She could, however, give the woman a hug and kiss on the cheek, so that was what she did.

Knock, knock.

The next door opened to reveal a fellow with a bright pink

dome. He was buttoning up his shirt. "Can't talk," he said. "I'm late for my bridge game. Thanks for holding the door."

She held the door a few moments longer than she needed to, and she could see that he had nothing hanging anywhere except a car mechanic's calendar by the bathroom door, open to September, although it was still April. The girl pictured thereupon, draped in bits of gauze, posing atop a stack of Italian tires, gazed boldly at her as if to say, *some art lovers appreciate ducks, farmhouses, and faux Gainsborough skies; this guy is not the first to prefer a nude.*

"King Francis the second of Spain couldn't get enough of them," Stella told the girl in the picture. With a feeling of good cheer, she let the door swing shut.

Knock, knock. Knock, Knock.

The last door in Fern Corridor, and the tone for lunch sounded, almost covering the sound of Stella's knock. When the tone stopped and Stella left off knocking, she heard in the sudden quiet a soft keening noise.

Stella called out, "Are you all right?" and the noise paused, but only for a moment.

"May I come in?" She pushed inside the room.

There, on the chair beside the bed, a woman sat naked, shivering, half-covered with a damp towel.

Stella hurried to the woman's side. "What happened here? You poor thing."

"I'm cold," the woman said.

"I'll bet you are." Stella dragged a blanket from the bed, and replaced the wet towel with the blanket. She flung the towel on top of the dresser by the washroom door. "What's your name, dear?" Stella winced, knowing how much she must sound like the Nameless Dear care workers.

"Ruby." The woman made no move to draw the blanket round her, and Stella did it for her.

"Ruby, where are your clothes?" Stella asked. "Did you just have a bath? Why did they leave you here in this state?"

Ruby gazed at her and made no answer.

Stella rose and searched through the dresser drawers, where socks and underwear were neatly rolled into sausages, the way Stella's always returned from the laundry room. She fished out the warmest-looking clothes she could find and dressed Ruby as she had once dressed her daughter Junie.

"Thank you," Ruby breathed. "How nice it must be to be able to do all these things, my dear."

"My name is Stella. Let me just put on your socks for you."

Stella got down onto one knee, and the other, and sat on the floor. She tugged woolly pink socks over Ruby's pale feet.

"Stella, Stella, it must be nice, so very nice … "

"What's that?" Stella used the end of the bed to stand up, feeling by this point quite breathless. "What would be nice, Ruby?"

"To be like you."

"Like me!" Stella's eyes filled with tears. She looked down into Ruby's eyes.

"Yes. Young, like you."

Stella took Ruby to the door, where a Nameless Dear rushed up and thanked her.

Stella was not about to accept the thanks. "Where were you?"

The nameless care worker frowned. "As a matter of fact, I was helping several more residents."

"Well, Ruby was cold, dangerously so, and needed help getting dressed. You might have put her at the top of the list."

"Then the others would have been cold and needing help," the care worker said crisply. "Thanks for your help, dear. We're late for lunch. Come along, Ruby."

Stella gazed after them as they moved slowly away from her. For a moment, she stood alone in the corridor, shivering, not with cold but with anger. Intimacy without affection was a terrible thing in any home, including Fairmount Manor.

Reliza appeared and moved towards her. "Stella, sure you know where you're going?"

"Of course I do."

Reliza took Stella by the shoulders and turned her round. "Straight ahead and then turn right, and you'll find the dining room. See you later."

Stella did not thank the girl. Nor did she follow Reliza's directions. She followed Reliza herself around the corner, to the spot where the effects closet faced the laundry room. The door to the laundry was just swinging shut, and Stella plunged through it after Reliza, just in time to see the door to the outside swing shut and click itself locked. She gazed from the door to the silent washing machines, to the stacks and stacks of cardboard boxes all around the room. It smelled oppressively soapy. She wished she could go after Reliza and get her opinion of Ruby's treatment by the nameless care worker. But Reliza was gone, off on whatever errands the world needed her to do, while Stella stood among the boxes and fumed.

It was just another example of how life went on without the elderly. They weren't allowed to follow where youth went. They were, however, allowed to make a fuss. It was a bit like ghosts were allowed to haunt buildings, moving things around, making dreadful sounds. Stella decided to report the nameless care worker who had left Ruby naked and shivering. She wouldn't stop until the woman was fired. Even Fairmount Manor had standards, and leaving old women in a state like that must violate the lowest of standards.

What kind of a defence had the woman made, telling Stella that others would be cold if she helped Ruby first?

Stella scowled. If she took her complaint to the Director, there were only two possible replies to her charge. The Director might say that

1. Stella was right, in which case the care worker would be fired, and then there would be one less person to help take care of Ruby;

or

2. Stella was entirely wrong, and the care worker would not be fired, in which case Ruby would be in the same situation tomorrow as she was today.

Stella wished that she could think of a third option. She could not. She could only curse, so she did, under her breath. And she could punch something — not the concrete wall, of course. Instead she punched at the nearest cardboard boxes, piled up to make a sort of wall. The wall fell. And she found herself staring into the face of her teenaged grandson, Junie's son, Derek.

CHAPTER FIVE

So tightly sealed was Stella's existence at Fairmount Manor that she could hardly believe her grandson Derek had found a way to enter it, and stood before her among the toppled cardboard boxes that had previously formed a wall. Stella took in the closet-sized space behind the cardboard boxes she had knocked down. A sleeping pallet made of grubby-looking duvets lay crumpled on the concrete floor. A cardboard box turned on end made a table holding what must have been Derek's lunch—a bag of potato chips yawning open beside a six-pack of cola. Stella smelled tomato and cheese before she made out the stack of pizza boxes near the head of the bed, with a paperback novel lying face down and open on top of the stack, as if it were a bedside table. She gaped at her grandson, whom she'd never felt able to love as a grandmother ought.

"Ye gods and little fishes!" Stella's cry was straight from her own teen years. "Derek, have you no sense at all?"

Derek scowled. "Hello, Gran."

"I'm furious with you." Stella clenched her fists in an effort to feel her own fury, but it was no use. She was so relieved to find him alive and unharmed and, above all wonders, not a ghost at all. "I've never been angrier in my life."

She moved toward him, and he took a step backward. She took two more steps forward and wrapped her arms around him. He was taller than she now. When he and Junie used to visit Stella, and he did nothing but stare at TV, Stella and he had been of a size. She pressed her face into the hollow of his shoulder and squeezed him tight.

He mumbled, "I didn't do anything to you."

"Not just me. It's your mother. She's … "

"When did you talk to her?"

"Well." Stella skated around the guilty truth with the same adeptness she'd employed to avoid her daughter's phone calls. "She must be out of her mind with worry, Derek."

He scowled. "My name isn't Derek."

"Yes, it is. I was present at your baptism." Stella had a sudden ghastly feeling that she was wrong after all, that her more recent memories, for example of her last fifteen years outside Fairmount, had been more dream than reality, and that Junie had decided to name her son something different and Stella had managed to forget the fact. "Fourteen years ago."

"He is sixteen." A girl's voice spoke up suddenly. "And it's true, his name isn't Derek."

Stella looked past Derek to see a familiar, if not very friendly, face. Edwina — the thief named Edge — stood behind Derek, hands on narrow teenaged hips.

Where had she come from?

Stella said, "Derek is a perfectly good name, and I'm going to call him that ... Edwina."

"Edge," Edwina corrected her. She picked up a fallen carton and stacked it atop another. Did the girl think to recreate Derek's hiding place? Did she think that, once discovered, the two of them could stay hidden? Teenagers strewed about them their own type of gaga, Stella reflected. And there was only one way to navigate gaga: you didn't argue, you just walked around it and tried not to get any on your shoe.

Edwina repeated, "Call me Edge, Gran."

"Mrs Ryman to you, Edwina." Stella saw the unfairness of it. "All right. *Edge. But* what exactly are you two doing ... ?"

Stella trailed off, suddenly aware of the contents of several boxes stacked about the untidy bed within the cardboard carton walls. They were full of objects. She made out a jumble of paperback books with a music box on top, a round cushion cover, several wash bags, and the sleeves of a knitted purple garment hanging out the top. Corners of framed photographs stuck up above the sides of the boxes, and they pictured happy families, none of them Derek's. A large plastic radio dating from at least four decades back sat on top of an upturned carton against the wall. And behind the radio, half-hidden in the shadows, the gleam of a faux-gold picture frame.

Now Stella did feel fury. The real thing, mounting in hot waves up her neck and cheeks to her ears. She pushed past Derek and Edge. She pointed. "This is … " She could hardly speak. "This picture is mine."

"I know." Derek shrugged.

"Don't you shrug your shoulders at me. You came in disguised as a ghost and took this picture out of my room." She picked up the picture by its frame, turning the farmyard, the cherry blossoms, and dear old ducks away from him. Nobody would ever love them as she did.

"You weren't using it," Derek said. "It wasn't even hung up properly, it was just sitting there for anybody to take."

"But why would they?" Stella raged. "Why would you?"

"I always liked it. I always looked at it for a long time, whenever I came to your house."

This surprising announcement took the wind out of Stella's sails. You never knew what was important to other people. But she puffed up her sails again when she realized that made no difference. She gestured from the picture to the other objects boxed up around her, Derek, and Edge. "You're a thief."

"There!" Edge cried. The delight in the girl's voice was unmistakable. "There you go. *Thief.*"

"Gran doesn't mean what you mean," Derek mumbled.

"I do," Stella said.

Edge hit Derek on the arm with her open hand. "His *name* is Thief. Like mine is Edge."

"Thief is a terrible name," Stella said. "Far worse than Derek."

Her grandson sighed. "I was going to be Aragorn son of Arathorn, but then I stole your picture. So I thought, what about being a Prince of Thieves?"

"Like mine is Edge."

"Because the edge is the line where everything disappears," Derek said.

Derek had it wrong. Fairmount Manor was the place where everything disappeared.

Stella set down her picture against the laundry room wall. She couldn't go one more minute without shaking her finger at them. "Of all the lowdown, dirty deeds, stealing from old people!"

"The things we took never left the building," Edge pointed out coldly. "That makes a big difference, legally speaking."

Stella was so angry she couldn't look at them. And that was when she spotted it: the corner of a shiny black box, just visible underneath a heap of mixed-up pyjama pieces in one of Derek's boxes of stolen property on the far side of his makeshift bed.

Stella advanced upon the box, set her picture down on the bed, and bent over with a hand to the concrete laundry room wall for support. She scooped the pyjamas out of the carton. She picked up the shiny black mah-jongg box that had once belonged to Thelma Hu and set it on the floor before her. Her fingers shook as she opened it. There was something inside. Not money. With set mouth, she snatched up from the box's interior the peach-coloured underwear that had formerly been her best item of lingerie. She tucked her underwear into her pocket and straightened up to face them.

"Now she's really mad," Edge observed.

Stella took a deep breath.

Edge, that place where everything disappears, and Derek, Prince of Thieves, met her gaze. Stella thought bitterly that this was a rotten time to discover that, whether a child was six or sixteen, some things did not disappear.

CHAPTER SIX

Stella sat upright on the second of three institution-style chairs set in a line in Fairmount's glassed-in foyer. In the third seat her grandson Derek squinted against the afternoon sun. The first chair stood empty. It remained to be revealed whether, when Stella's daughter Junie arrived, she would sit down in it to scold Derek and Stella, or whether she would give voice from a standing position.

Stella tightened her grip on the mah-jongg box in her lap and caught Derek's sideways glance. He seemed smaller since Edge had left for her own home. He looked very young to be Prince of Thieves. She put a hand on his shoulder. In the receptionist's cubicle a few feet away, she caught sight of a nameless care worker gazing at the two of them, grandmother and grandson. Was she thinking that it was very nice indeed for a young fellow in his teens to visit his elder relation? Or perhaps she had spoken to Junie and was thinking to herself, *they are an unlikely pair of ne'er-do-wells.*

For *ne'er-do-wells* was the epithet that Junie had let loose overtop Stella's attempt at explaining Derek's presence here at Fairmount. *Do you mean to say that he sat on the foot of your bed every night for a week and you never thought to call me? Have you completely forgotten how it feels to be a mother, Mother?*

"I thought he was a ghost," Stella had answered her. But even to herself, the explanation sounded feeble, so that when Junie started shouting down the line, Stella endured it as a sort of penance. In the end, the penance done, but the hollering still going on, Stella had handed the phone back to Reliza, who after one doubtful look held the receiver away from her head and was still doing so when Stella walked off, mah-jongg box tucked under her arm, to her own Room 34, to lie down while Junie flew the three thousand miles it would take to get her here.

Now Derek, who had drooped his longish hair over packet soup, bread, and butter for lunch with Fairmount's residents, sat with Stella and waited for Junie to arrive.

"Did you get enough lunch?" she asked Derek.

"I hate soup," Derek answered.

"I guess that must mean yes," Stella said. She attempted a smile. It felt stiff on her face, like waxed paper. "Whatever possessed you to come to Fairmount?" It was the third time she'd asked the question. The first two times he had shrugged at her. "I only ask because your mother is coming soon and we should get our stories straight."

He stopped mid-shrug. "I hate it at home. She's always somewhere else working, and she checks me on GPS because I'm grounded. I've been grounded for a month. For no reason."

Stella nodded. "That does sound unfair. However, I have a little experience with these things, and I must ask: no reason at all?"

"*No.* Well, shoplifting. Big deal. Even *she* said it was a cry for attention."

"Unsuccessful, I take it?"

He scowled. "It woke *me* up, anyway. I don't have to stay there. I'm grown-up enough, and I can get a job. By law."

"What job?" Stella asked.

"You're just the same as Mom. *What job, what job?* Well, I couldn't get one after all. So I took off."

Stella leaned a couple of inches over so that she could see the clock on in the reception cubicle wall. Junie ought to be there by now. Perhaps she'd missed her plane and would have to await the next. Stella pictured Junie in a temper. She looked down at the box in her lap.

Derek said, "I came all this way to see you, Gran, and when I sat on your bed all you did was cover up your head. So I went and lived in the laundry. It was very boring until I met Edge on her school visit."

The Prince of Thieves. Outside the foyer door Stella caught sight of movement. Was that a taxi? No, just somebody turning a minivan around with swift precision in Fairmount's driveway and heading off again with a roar. Stella decided to take a lesson from the minivan.

She stood up and tucked the mah-jongg box under her arm. "Look, Prince of Thieves. I'm too old to be shouted at by anybody I fed and diapered. Will you please deal with your mother for both of us?"

"That doesn't seem fair at all."

"I think it does, dear. And here's why. You're not otherwise occupied."

Derek looked from the foyer doors to the corridor crossing to the reception cubicle, his lanky bangs swinging a little with the movement.

"Meanwhile, I do have something important to attend to." Stella hesitated. "Come see me any time. In the daylight, mind you."

"Ha, ha," Derek said. But he sounded a little more cheerful.

Stella was not surprised. She felt a little more chipper herself. This was because

1. she loved her grandson better than she ever had before, and that was because

2. his coming here showed that he loved her better than she'd ever dreamed, and,

3. she had found throughout her teaching career that most kids liked to be heroes if they got a chance.

The Prince of Thieves muttered, "You're going to have to deal with her at some point."

For a reply Stella gave him a kiss on the head, the first kiss since he was small that he'd received from her without flinching. Then she turned her back on him and the three institutional-style chairs, and walked away from the glass foyer door through which Junie would soon enter.

CHAPTER SEVEN

Mid-afternoon was prime time for napping, and Stella was pleased to see that while the Greek Chorus was not present, Thelma sat in her usual chair in Corridor Park. Careful not to drop her treasure, Stella sat down in her seat under the skylight. She negotiated her way around Thelma's cane, held as always in both hands, to set the mah-jongg box on Thelma's bony, black-trousered lap.

"There. Look what I found, while I was sleuthing around."

Thelma only scowled, which was completely the wrong reaction. But Stella was so pleased to have found Thelma's box, it was no hardship just now to soldier on. She took the cane from Thelma. She accepted the resultant dark mutterings as part of the scenery of the moment. She took both Thelma's hands—frail, light, and cool as seashells—and placed them on the smooth lacquered lid of the box.

"What is this?" Thelma hissed.

"You know what this is." Stella crushed a laugh of triumph before it could make itself heard.

"Do I?"

"I kept my promise."

"Did you?"

"I found your mah-jongg box."

The explanation should have been unnecessary, but *should* was a word lacking its full traditional import here at Fairmount Manor. Stella added, "I must admit that I didn't find it entirely through deduction. I had some good luck too."

"This is not my box."

Thelma flattened her hands on its top.

Stella braced herself for battle. "It's your black lacquer mah-jongg box."

"It's not."

"It's exactly how you described the box to me."

Nope," Thelma said.

"But—"

"I had my box for fifty years. Sixty. I think I'd know it if this was it."

Stella sat back in her chair. So much of soldiering on in a care home — surrounded by the uncertainty of whether one would actually wake up in the morning to a new day, and whether one even wanted to wake up to it — was keeping up with changes in perspective. For wasn't a search like hers a part of every search, even great quests like the hunt for the Grail? And Don Quixote's search for his perfect lover? And the whole point of those stories was that neither King Arthur, Don Quixote, Grail, or Dulcinea were as important as the purity of the final goal. Her eyes pricked with tears. She trusted that they were tears of happiness.

Thelma opened the box. She moved her hands around inside it and angled her head to see inside it with what little sight remained her. Then she closed it again, and tapped her nails on the box's lid. "This is a mystery for you to solve. This is the Mystery of the Mah-Jongg Box."

"I've already solved it, for here it is."

"No. You found ... " Thelma scowled. "There's a word for it in grammar. You're a schoolteacher. What is the word?"

Stella remembered Thurber's essay on grammar, the reverse example for what Thelma was referencing. *She hit him with the milk* was an example of *the thing contained for the container.* "The container for the thing contained."

"Yes. You are mixing up the box and what the box contained. I want my money!" With a flourish, she pushed it off her lap. The box landed on the floor to splay open in front of Thelma's red silk slippers. One of the hinges snapped.

Thelma said. "See, it's empty. But I'm kind of glad."

"Thelma Hu, did you send me on a wild goose chase?"

"Certainly not!" Thelma sat up straight. "I want my damn

money that was in that box. And it's still up to you to find it."

"Then why are you glad I didn't find it yet?"

"I don't want to tell you why."

"Why not tell me why?" Stella felt the corner of her mouth quirk up. "Don't tell me. I know. It's the mystery of it. You don't want it to be over. You don't want the mystery to end."

"That's not it at all," Thelma said.

"Then what?"

Thelma made a grumpy noise.

Stella said, "That cranky sound reminds me that I've got to go."

"I heard your daughter is here."

"Yes." Stella sighed. The best way not to be lonely was to need nobody. That sounded as true as any song lyric, and as false as any lie you told yourself when you could not sleep at night in your care home bed. She gazed up through the skylight at the pearly sky above Fairmount. "I had better get moving."

"Will you come back once you've seen your daughter?" Thelma asked.

"Why wouldn't I?"

"Maybe she'll want you to go with her?"

"She lives in a tiny apartment, just her and my grandson Derek. Three thousand miles away," Stella said. "But Thelma, I must say that now, when my family is mad at me, it's good to have a friend to count on when I get back."

"Don't count on too much," Thelma said. "I'm no spring chicken. I might not be here when you get back."

"See you later." Stella rose and walked out of Corridor Park, turning right, then left, and right again, walking at a steady pace. There would be a scolding. There would be blame and imprecations. Still, a lifetime of emergency school staff meetings had taught her to stand against the wind when it blew. When one attended any sort of meeting, one must know what one wanted to achieve, and Stella would be damned if she'd let Junie get away from their first meeting in six months without a long hard hug and a kiss.

Her heart moving far more quickly than her footsteps, Stella set out to meet her daughter.

§

For more of Stella's adventures pick up the full-length novel, Stella Ryman and the Fairmount Manor Mysteries. *Available from Pulp Literature Press and Amazon.com*

CLEARING OUT NESTS

Brandon Crilly

An Ottawa teacher by day, **Brandon Crilly** has been previously published by On Spec, The 2017 Young Explorer's Adventure Guide, Third Flatiron Anthologies *and other markets. He received an Honourable Mention in the 2016 Writer's Digest Popular Fiction Awards, contributes regularly to BlackGate. com, and develops programming for Can-Con in Ottawa. You can find Brandon at brandoncrilly.wordpress.com or @B_Crilly.*

CLEARING OUT NESTS

Hana triple-checked that she had cleaned all the dried blood off her skin before she left the restroom. No one in the coffee shop had noticed it when she walked in, so focused were they on their conversations or smart phones. There had only been a few patches of gore; she thought about sitting down at the counter to see how long it took for someone to give her a weird look. Or scream. Willis would have killed her if she'd tried that, though, so her bloody hijab, shirt and pants went into her backpack, to join the pile of similar laundry waiting at home.

A steaming cup of coffee was waiting for her at the long counter that looked out on the street. Willis had a newspaper in front of him, but that was just for show; between sips of herbal tea, his eyes were on the empty building across the street, one hand resting near the duffel bag that held their weapons. The place across the street had been a clothing store before a couple of unexplained deaths led to it closing down. There was a gap in the polite FOR LEASE signs lining the windows, but if no one had seen Hana take it down with her when one of the ghouls threw her across the interior, she doubted anyone would bat an eye now.

"Nothing, I'm guessing?" Hana asked.

"Not a peep."

Hana took a careful sip of coffee, but the motion still made her throat ache where that ghoul had grabbed her. She grimaced, and Willis shook his head.

"Please don't start already."

"You should've gone left," he said. He licked drips of tea from his shock-white mustache.

"Are you really going to criticize me for making the wrong choice on a fifty-fifty chance? If you thought I should've gone left, maybe you could've shouted or something, because going right seemed perfectly fine to me at the time."

Willis grunted. "You're being too loud."

"Like anyone would care," Hana murmured. She glanced around. The patrons in here had been two lanes of traffic away from a nest of ghouls that would have gladly ripped their faces off and danced in their skin. But of course they had no clue, and would go on with their blissfully ignorant lives, thanks to people like Hana and Willis.

In fact ... She looked past the tables and signs advertising fancy coffee to examine the coffee shop's basic layout.

"Have we been here before?"

Willis's eyes shifted slightly to study the reflection in the window, while he kept half his attention on the other building.

"We have. Cleared this place about ... eight months ago, or something."

"Huh." Hana frowned. This had been something else before it was a coffee shop — sporting goods, maybe, before the ghouls moved into the basement? "Didn't take them long to stake a claim." As though the city needed another place like this.

It was one of those chains that seemed to show up on every street corner.

"Capitalism," Willis said, like that answered everything.

Hana decided her throat hurt too much to keep talking and focused on her overpriced coffee.

She didn't see Willis for another two weeks. They weren't exactly friends, after all; just workmates, sort of, within their secret world. He had told her a long time ago that being seen together elsewhere would just lead to questions no one wanted to answer.

Of course, that didn't stop him from calling her while she was preparing to read the Friday prayer. She told him he had the worst timing ever — he knew — and that the job would have to wait, because her parents would kill her if she "abandoned her responsibility." He was wise enough not to make some comment about Allah not caring where she was. But he was not above describing the four teenagers who had been gutted the night before behind one of those youth hangout clubs designed as a safe space for underage kids. Hana grumbled something that would have earned a stern lecture from her parents, and endured a lesser one when she told them she wasn't feeling well enough to read. She waited for them to drive off then called Willis to come pick her up.

When the last ghoul came at her this time, Hana ducked left. Gray flesh, gnashing teeth and wicked claws sailed past her, denting a vending machine on their way to the ground. The machine only dispensed zero-calorie drinks and flavoured water, so Hana had no issue tearing it apart with her shotgun as she put down the ghoul.

Willis stepped up to her, gore dripping from his mustache and past his grin. "What did I say? Always duck left."

Hana checked her hijab for blood, saw a few splotches as always, and flipped him off.

They cleaned up before the walk back to Willis's car; he never parked close to the nest they were clearing. While they waited on a street corner for the light to change, Hana contemplated an overpriced coffee, but shook her head. She needed to get home before her parents. Besides, there were enough coffee shops near her house —

When the light changed she didn't move, and Willis had to backpedal several steps to rejoin her. "What's up?"

Hana looked from the coffee shop — where she had changed from her bloody clothes two weeks earlier — and pointed across the street. The FOR LEASE signs were gone from the empty building they had cleared. In their place were brighter, larger signs proclaiming COMING SOON, with the name of a coffee chain. The same chain as the place right beside her.

"You were right," Willis said. "They don't take long to stake a claim."

"Yeah." The light changed again, but Hana still didn't move, thinking about the coffee shop that used to be a clothing store, and the one that used to sell sporting goods or something. "Willis, you don't think ... "

Willis laughed. "Just capitalism. You religious people and your imaginations ... "

The comment got her hackles up, and by the time she'd finished chewing him out, she had forgotten her suspicions.

Three weeks later, the youth hangout they'd cleared was slated to start selling overpriced coffee.

LOVE

Greg Brown

Greg Brown *is a graduate of the MFA program in Creative Writing at the University of North Carolina-Greensboro. He is a recipient of UBC's Roy Daniels Memorial Essay Prize, and you can find his stories, criticism, and essays in* Postscript, Paragon, The RS500, Lenses: Perspectives on Literature, *and* Tate Street. *His surreal short story 'Bear' appeared in* Pulp Literature Issue 14.

$\mathscr{L}$OVE

We agreed as a family that the only thing to do was to bring Mom home for the next few months or weeks, whatever it would be. It'll be hard, Dad said. But maybe it can be fine, too. Denisa was suspicious about the cost of it all—like the private nurse we'd have to pay for, where at the hospital it was free—although she didn't put it like that, said that we'd be crazy to bring Mom into a place where there wasn't any immediate care, because what if there was a problem like before, the thing with her stent that plugged up and caused some internal bleeding that almost wasn't staunched in time?

She *could've*, Denisa said.

The oncologist had said October, and the late pale fog had come and now the sky was mostly dimmed and gone by suppertime.

I said that I would only do it if we agreed that Pastor Karen would not come to the house; I was not comfortable with Pastor Karen coming to the house. Jon and Dad looked at me a moment and said, Okay.

Denisa said, I don't get what you don't like about Pastor Karen.

And I explained why I didn't like Pastor Karen.

And Denisa said, Well I don't think it's really fair to call her a liar.

And I explained why I thought it *was* fair to call Pastor Karen a liar.

And Denisa said, Well, by that standard they're all liars. And then we'd all be liars, too. The whole thing would be a lie. We don't need lies right now.

And I agreed with Denisa, especially about how we didn't need lies right now.

And Denisa said, It doesn't matter, because who cares what we know and don't know. If mom wants her to visit, then she visits.

I said, I care.

And Denisa said, You're unbelievable.

The family counsellor in the palliative care ward arranged for the hospital to loan us one of their extra beds, and then one of the RNs in the palliative care ward arranged for a delivery service to bring the bed by and for the ambulance service to drive Mom from the hospital. We watched, standing far clear of the foyer, uncertain about how wide a berth to give, as the ambulance attendants bounced the gurney over the uneven tile in the kitchen.

You're home, Dad said, as the attendants rolled Mom from the gurney into the special hospital bed. Mom looked up and smiled and didn't say anything.

She passed very early the next morning, and Dad woke us up to tell us what had happened. That he'd gone into her room to help her with her bedpan and that he'd found her very still, nothing going into her and nothing coming out. I don't know why he said it like that: "Nothing going into her and nothing coming out." Then he said that he'd already called the hospital and spoken with Dr Halford and that Dr Halford said that the hospital would send over the ambulance and he reminded Dad about the paperwork that he would need to have at hand because the coroner would also be over with the ambulance because it was protocol for the coroner to check in to make sure that we had the right kind of permits for the deceased. I don't know why Dad told us all of this, we didn't need to know it.

There isn't a lot of time, Dad said, before they'll be here to take her, and I think you should each take a moment.

We would take turns sitting with the body in the bedroom—if it was just that, a body—where it was still prone in the borrowed hospital bed, where nothing was going into it and nothing coming out.

First, it was Jon's turn since he was the youngest and that seemed fair and important to honour. The rest of us sat in the living room where we hadn't yet taken down the Christmas decorations and listened, but also did not listen, to the sounds that were coming out of the bedroom. We looked at the Christmas tree because there was nothing else to look at and because it was there and because we'd forgotten to take it down. We'd done a very good job decorating it, even though we'd used many homemade decorations—gingerbread men with purple silk looped through their head-holes and chains of old popcorn threaded with green fishing line. I don't like homemade decorations because they look sloppy and cheap and often like they are made by children as these ones were since of course we'd made them as children many, many years ago. But I thought the tree looked almost fine.

We could hear Jon speaking, but I tried not to hear it and I clenched my jaw just tightly enough to aggravate the ringing in my left ear. But the tree looked fine even with the ringing in my ear and Jon's quiet noises and my only real regret about the tree was the winged, brass treetopper — which actually was store bought, not handmade by us as children — which was canted at the top of the tree either because the last tree spoke or whatever you call the top branch was bent or because Jon, who'd been the one to put it on top of the tree, had put it on in a hurry although that didn't seem very likely, he was careful mostly.

Jon came out and he was wiping his nose with the collar of his shirt. He sat down beside Dad and Dad put an arm around him and then they leaned their heads together, almost like they were in love.

Then Denisa stood up and said, There's no way.

And Dad said, You won't get another chance.

And Denisa said, I don't want to remember any of this. And then Denisa sat back down and covered her face with one of the Christmas throw pillows.

In the bedroom, there was the body still in the bed, nothing going into it. Her eyes shone brightly, still full of wet surprise and I wondered if she was *actually*. I stood beside the borrowed hospital bed which had been brought into our house and I stood and looked down at her, the body. There was nothing to do or to say. I remembered that before, when she was in the hospital, she wasn't always lucid. She dreamed while she was awake — that's how Dr Halford explained it — and talked through the dreams as they appeared to her. I remembered that in one dream it was like she was a small child. It seemed like somebody was angry at her, like she'd done something wrong. I stood and listened for a while.

I won't say it, she said. It's poison to say it. Jon is sick because he said the words. He has a fever and I don't want to catch the fever. This school is a bad school. This school makes you sick if you say the words.

I became scared and left the room and found one of the nurses and told her what was happening. When we got back to the room she was still talking, but she seemed better.

Would you put another log on the fire, dear, Mom said. It's very cold.

The nurse said, Of course, darling, let me see what's left of the cord out back. And then mom was quiet for a while and the nurse said to me, I hope you don't mind about that. And even though I was angry because I don't believe in lying, I didn't say anything.

And weeks later — she was in the hospital for so long — she woke up in the early evening and she said to me, Oh, there are angels outside the door. I hear them. They're saying that they're here for me. They're here to heal me. To make me better. They say that I'm cured. And I said, Mom, no. And she said, Open the door. And I said, Please, stop. And she said, You're not listening to me. The angels are here, you've got to let them in before they leave. Stop, I said. She said, You don't make them wait. And I said, Look the door is open and where are the angels? She leaned out of her bed, wincing or searching I couldn't say. Her body was so small and yellow and slow. She stared at the empty doorway and then lay back down. You're right, she whispered. There's nothing. I'm sorry.

It's fine, I said.

THE OLDE TOWN HAUNT

Patrick Bollivar

Patrick Bollivar *is a writer and an air traffic controller living in Vancouver, BC. His short stories have previously appeared in* Tesseracts Nineteen: Superhero Universe, The Outliers of Speculative Fiction, *and* Pulp Literature *Issue 10, under the earlier pen name PE Bolivar.*

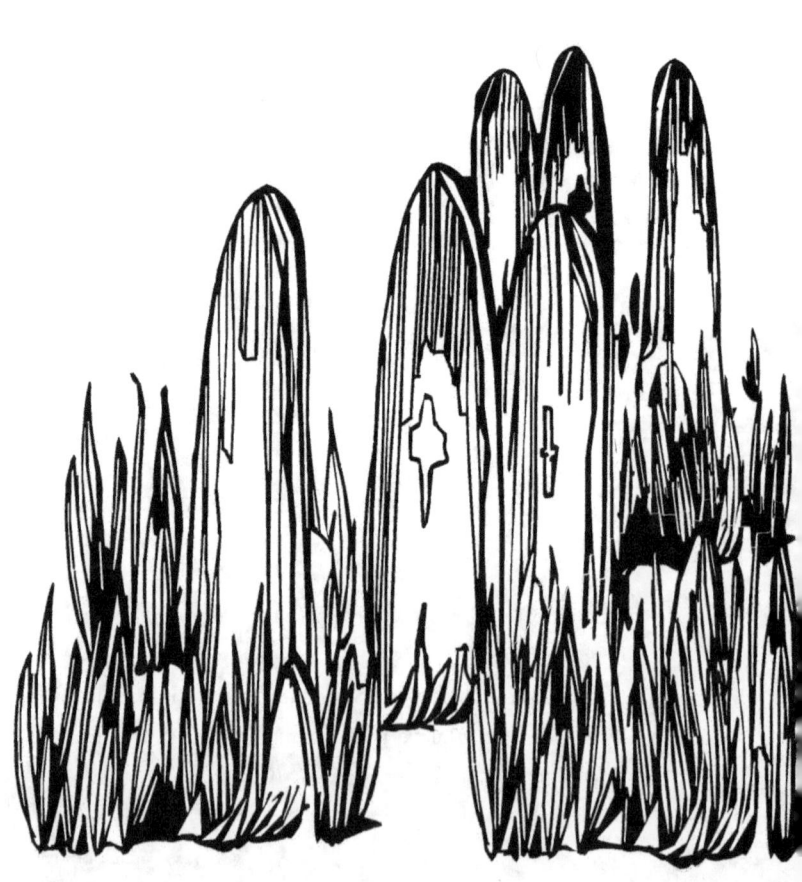

The Olde Town Haunt

Ghosts can be hungry, but there is none hungrier than the *è guǐ*. He is a nightmare, and his hunger eats people alive.

My mother knew this, had warned me many times about him. "Beware, my little rice girl," she said. "He is *xié'è*, a devil roaming amongst friendlier spirits. He has charm, and he will promise you the moon in the sky, but the only reward you'll receive from him is a quick trip to the underworld."

If only my mom had listened to her own warnings. But then, she was never the same after the car accident.

I woke to the sound of my baby brother wailing like a banshee from his corner of the room. I threw my pillow in his general direction. That only made his wail grow louder, something I hadn't even dreamt possible. "Jai, shut up! Mom! Mom, he's at it again!" When I received no answer, my heart tripped over itself with worry.

I scrambled out of bed, my body shuddering at being forced out from under my warm comforter into the chill of the room. I threw on yesterday's clothes—a frayed plaid skirt, thick black tights full of runs, an even thicker sweater — before heading to the bedroom door.

In the living room of our small apartment, I discovered why it was so cold. The sliding glass door sat open, letting in the January air. "Crap on a stick," I said before closing it. I checked Mom's room and found the bed made, the corners crisply tucked the way she liked it done every morning. She must have passed out in Dad's old chair again. It lay empty now, next to the side table where she kept her medicine bottles. They were knocked over, the pills strewn across the carpet, some ground to dust. She must have stepped on them as she staggered into the night.

I grabbed my satchel and filled it with a container of rice leftover from dinner, some fruit, incense sticks, a lighter, and my lumpy welder goggles. After stuffing my tangled hair up under my tuque, I pulled on fingerless gloves and black hiking boots then headed back in to see Jaiden. "Calm down, Jai. I'll go get her. Be back soon, I promise." Jaiden's shrieks shrunk to mewling cries, a sound so pitiful it broke my heart.

I paused at the front door beside the portrait of Zhong Kui, the Demon Queller. His fierce face and comical beard stared back at me. "Keep him safe, please," I said before heading outside and locking the apartment behind me.

More cold hit me as soon as I left the shelter of the co-op. I fought the desire to run back inside, back under my warm blanket. The smell of cedar logs burnt the air, bitterly reminding me of a warm, crackling fire. Someone was at home next to a cosy blaze. *Wish it were me.* Wrapping my arms tight, I set off, following in my mother's footsteps.

I snorted at the thought. Following in her footsteps was the last thing I wanted to do. Mom was *mun mai poh*, a Chinese medium. Unfortunately, it ran in the family. Well, I wanted none of it. Being a medium sucked. Sure, you could speak with the dead, but so what? They never had anything interesting to say.

I crossed the road to the cemetery, but stopped before my feet entered the grounds. The haze lay thick here. The streetlights barely shone through it, giving the dark night the gleam of a cheesy painting, the kind found at IKEA with LED lights built into the canvas to give boring cityscapes a smidge of character. I hated those things, and I hated the fact that I was about to walk through the graveyard on a night like this.

I could already hear them moaning beside their headstones. They always knew whenever me or my mom was near. Out of my satchel I pulled my welder's goggles. The glass in them was special, too thick for regular frames. A gift to my mother from a ghost catcher she'd helped once, they helped me see what I could normally only hear. As I slipped them on, I tried not to think about how ridiculous they made me look. With a deep breath, I entered the cemetery.

Shadows appeared to me in the haze, *hun* spirits hovering over their own graves, moaning about their deaths. My heart beat quickly as I pulled my iPod out, shoved in the ear buds, and cranked up the volume. Florence and the Machine began to howl 'Shake It Out' in my ears, boosting my confidence as I half-jogged, half-danced my way between the spirits, doing my best to avoid their touch. Music kept their complaints from worming into my brain, and kept me from swatting at them like buzzing flies, something I'd seen my mother do on her worst days.

Only those too stubborn to accept their passing stuck around, so the voices I heard tended to do nothing but bitch and complain. Bunch of whiners, really. It was the angry ones that I wanted to avoid the most. They had the power to drain a medium if they got their psychic hooks in you. The goggles came in handy whenever I needed to beat a hasty retreat. Can't run from what I can't see.

Instead of running away from them, tonight I walked towards the dead, just like my mom had done all her life. She called it a gift, or at least she used to, before she crashed our car on the Upper Levels Highway, damaging her head, her back, and worse, her soul. Now she only spoke with the dead alone, at night, singing soft songs to quiet my brother while the other ghosts lingered beyond our doors. Sometimes their calls would be too much for her to resist, and she'd go to them. My little bro Jaiden always knew when she left, and because of him, so did I.

Mom hadn't been the only person in that car crash. My baby brother still didn't realize he'd died that day.

Taking out my ear buds for a moment, I called out, "Mom!" The calm night carried my words away from me, offering no reply. Mountain View stretched for six blocks from east to west and ten blocks north to south. If she'd wandered in here it could be ages before I found her. Few lights broke up the blackness inside, the fog as thick as molasses along the wide stretches of grass.

I'd need some help, help I really didn't want, but you know, desperate times ...

A short walk into the less populated corner of Mountain View got me to the headstone I searched for. Hanging around it, singing softly to himself, shimmered a ghost about my age, fifteen, sixteen, tops. He'd died in the eighties, and it showed. His black leather jacket had spikes to match his Billy Idol hair. Upon seeing me, he gave a spin and danced a little on his heels, his pale, translucent face shining with drops of moonlight. When he turned around, I caught a glimpse of the wound on the back of his head that had done him in.

"Hey, if it isn't my babe, Charlotte! How's Ms Tan on this fine evening?"

"Not great, Fang, otherwise I wouldn't be here, would I?" Fang Lau had found me during last year's Hungry Ghost Festival and followed me that whole month in an attempt to get me to exact revenge on his killers. Fang had run with a bad crowd in high school and paid for it with a baseball bat to the parietal lobe. I'd feel sorry for him if he wasn't so annoying. "Have you seen my mother?"

"Depends. What's in it for me? Ready to try some ghost love, *Lang Nui*? Let's get it on, *Ghostbusters* style."

Ignoring him, I opened my satchel and pulled out a couple of bowls, which I quietly placed near his headstone and filled with rice and fruit. I lit incense sticks and offered a moment of prayer. The cocky grin he'd been sporting earlier faded, replaced with a look of hunger.

"*Do jeh.* It's been so long."

"I know, Fang. But you are remembered. Please, will you help me?"

He nodded his head and told me which way she'd gone. In thanks, I burned joss paper marked with symbols of joy and happiness. Billy Idol sang 'Rebel Yell' on my iPod while the paper danced into the air and disappeared into smoke.

I left the cemetery and ran down the hill towards Main Street, the yellow haze of the streetlights my only company. As I approached the rundown mall on the corner, I could hear music drifting on the air. I slowed down and listened, catching snippets of laughter and conversation through the glass windows up ahead. Normal people would have heard the noise as whispers upon the wind, but to me the sounds were like nails on a blackboard, sending an icy chill through me. I should have gone pee before leaving the apartment.

The windows belonged to the abandoned pub at the back of the mall, the black glass etched with images of Victorian men and women sitting at tables, joyfully imbibing alcoholic spirits. The Penny Lane had closed the year before, and now it was the favourite haunt of wandering *guǐ*, the most unsettled of *hun*. The thought that my mom might be in there sent spasms through my stomach.

The glass of the pub's front door had been smashed, replaced by wooden boards. I tried to open it, but it wouldn't budge. Bracing my shoulder against the wood, I gave a good shove, tumbling into the pub ungracefully.

The music stopped as I hit the floor. The entranceway carpet smelled of mildew, the air of cigarette smoke. Beyond the carpet lay hardwood floor, covered in circular white marks where tables used to be. Those that remained were upturned, their chairs broken. The bar was cracked and peeling, the brass rail and taps gone. The large mirror behind the bar had been marked by a graffiti tag of yellow, dripping paint. No wonder the owner of the mall had trouble finding new tenants.

I could hear the clear ring of glasses chiming against each other followed by whispers of conversation, but the spirits that made these sounds were nowhere to be seen. My goggles had slid onto my forehead when I fell. I placed them back on, and the world changed.

"Classy joint," I said to the crowd watching me. The interior transformed before my eyes into a sparkling nightclub tinged in sepia gold. The spirits on the polished dance floor appeared alive but for their dark eyes and slightly shimmering forms. Their lithe bodies stood frozen mid-swing as they watched me. Three black jazz musicians and a white singer sat on the stage behind them. The singer was dressed in twenties flapper wear, ankles primly crossed, her whole body glowing under a white spotlight.

I got up, dusting myself off. The singer gave me a wink and continued her song. As the musicians began to play again, the dancers started moving in perfect sync, my presence quickly forgotten.

The place was crowded and loud, the corners lined with booths full of men talking up a storm over beers while women sat together at high tables where they could show off their legs and not crinkle their dresses. The whole place seemed like something out of a movie from the forties, though their clothes dated from much earlier: fedoras, high-collared shirts, and double-breasted vests. Girls with short hair, long lashes, and longer cigarette holders.

At first glance I saw no sign of Mom. The bar was crowded with men, cigarettes in every hand, some wearing black tuxes, some white, not a drop of colour among them. They glared at me through a cloud of tobacco smoke, dead eyes gazing out of pale cheeks.

I decided to search the booths at the back first and wove my way through the dance floor, feeling the occasional bump from the spinning couples as I went.

I exited the dance floor, ducking quickly under the tray of a waitress carrying drinks and cigarettes. The move went from graceful to clumsy as I tripped over a step and bumped into the nearest table.

"Steady on there, child," said a stout, round man whose brow seemed set in a permanent furrow. He had a moustache shooting down from his nose like the wings of a fighter jet. Two well dressed men sat beside him, also wearing various styles of soup strainers on their upper lips. I made my apologies and got ready to move on, but I was stopped by a hand. "Perhaps you could settle something for us," the stout man said. "Cope here claims he was a better mayor than I. But he went off chasing gold in the Klondike while I stayed true to this city, coaxing the gold right to our door!"

"I brought the Canada-Australia steam line to our shore," Mayor Cope replied vigorously. His moustache was bushier than the other two and flecked with gold. "All you truly did, Mayor Garden, was bring about the suicide of your electoral opponent!"

"I wouldn't know anything about that," I said, stepping away. The third man at the table grasped my hand before I could escape, clutching it in his grip.

"I did not kill myself," he said, staring glumly at me. He sat hunched over his glass of beer, his droopy moustache creating a picture of sadness. "Tell the historians that, would you? Set the record straight for me. It was him, he did it." His thumb jabbed towards the mayor with the jet fighter 'stache.

Mayor Garden furrowed his brow even further upon hearing the comment. "Don't listen to William, child! The honourable Mr Templeton here is still smarting over the thrashing I gave him back '98. Am I to blame that he doesn't know how many sleeping pills to take for a good night's rest?"

"Oh, he had a good rest all right!" said Mayor Cope with a bark.

The two men laughed, but not Mayor Templeton. "You should leave, girl," he whispered as he pulled me closer, his despairing eyes staring deep into mine. "Your young morals are in danger. Something hungry lies in wait upon the dance floor, or so I hear."

"Thanks. I'll keep that in mind," I said, trying to release my hand. His nails dug into my flesh, bringing up blood. "Stop it. You're hurting me!" I tore free, quickly backing away from the dead men. They shrugged as if nothing had happened and went back to their argument. Politicians, I thought with revulsion. They refused to die more than most.

"Pardon me, miss," said a tall man by my shoulder. His shoulders were ridiculously broad, almost bursting out of his fireman's uniform. He held two mugs of beer in one hand, a glass of water in the other. His black beard appeared to be made from soot. I quickly stepped aside to let him pass. He thanked me and continued towards a booth a few tables down. I followed.

He handed one of the beers to a fireman that could have been his twin—same sooty beard and all. A third man reached out from the back of the booth to take the glass of water. The sight of his arm made me scrunch my nose in disgust. It smoked, the skin black and crusted like a log that had spent a long time on the fire. I smelled cooking flesh and watched as flames occasionally licked across his arm.

The fireman noticed my stare. "Don't mind him, miss. He means no harm. Just thirsty is all."

As I got closer, I tried not to retch at the sight before me. The man's whole body was a smouldering ruin. His eyes looked like lit coals, the kind my dad used to use on our old hibachi BBQ.

A wind blew from out of nowhere, causing ash to drift off his head, taking parts of his scalp with it. He lifted the glass, swallowing the water in one long gulp. Parts of the fire receded, revealing a young man, red hair, a nice smile. It didn't last. The flames quickly engulfed him again, turning his face to blackened meat once more.

"What happened to him?"

"Fire of 1886. Burned from Main Street to Cambie. He blows in here once in awhile, nothing more than ash on the wind. Only wants water." The smouldering man gestured with his empty glass. The fireman nudged his friend. "Your turn, Joe."

Joe rolled his eyes before downing half his beer in one gulp. "You'll never quench it kid, even if you drink the whole ocean." He got up, disappearing into the crowd, glass in hand.

"Have you seen my mom?" I asked the remaining fireman. "A Chinese lady, probably wearing a bathrobe."

"Can't say I have."

After thanking him I moved on down the line, asking a group of Chinese railway workers at one table, then a booth full of prospectors that appeared to have frozen to death at the next. None had seen her.

When I reached the end of the room I was at my wits' end. What if she wasn't here at all? Where else could she have gone?

"Charlotte Tan, what are you doing here?" said a man behind me.

I turned to find David Robinson standing there in a dark charcoal suit and bowler hat. His face was chalk pale but for a golden sea star clasped to his cheek. His electric blue eyes crackled like lightning in a bottle.

Mr Robinson had been the wireless operator on the SS *Sophia*, a passenger liner that got stranded on Alaskan rocks a hundred years ago. The ship had sunk to the bottom of the ocean before help could arrive. The last voice the rescue ships heard came from this young man, before he froze to death.

He was also the first ghost I ever heard.

When I was ten, we lived in a nice townhouse off Oak Street paid for through my mother's work as a medium and Dad's job at the garage. I loved it there. The side streets were lined with cherry blossoms in the spring and the nearby playground was always filled with kids. Some would even play with the strange girl with the stranger mom.

One day I came home from school to find her in the kitchen, sitting with a nervous-looking man in a blue suit. They were listening to something on his phone, a recording of static by the sound of it.

"*Mah ma*, what are you doing?" I asked. Dad washed dishes in the sink nearby, scrubbing hard at a pot that already appeared clean to me.

"Shhh, Charlotte," said Mom. "Play it again, Mr Wong, louder. You're right to think there's a voice trying to be heard through the static."

"Is it a ghost, *Mah ma*?"

"This is none of your business, Charlotte," said my father crossly. "Go upstairs and do your homework."

"Hush, George," said Mom. "Let her stay. This is Mr Wong, from CKZZ. Their radio station is having static problems that none of their engineers can figure out. So he has come to me."

She nodded at Mr Wong, who played the recording once more. Loud static crackled over the speaker, along with something else.

"Why is that man so sad?" I asked.

My mother smiled at me. "Can you understand him, Charlotte?"

I nodded. "He's calling for a girl named Kyoko. He misses her."

Before my mother could answer, my father threw the SOS pad into the dirty water and stormed off.

With my help, Mom tracked down Kyoko. She'd been a young Japanese woman on board the Sophia whose body had never been recovered. We found her *hun* wandering along the northern BC shoreline and brought her back to Vancouver to be with David.

Kyoko floated beside him now, her hair billowing like seaweed on the ocean floor, her large eyes watching me intently. She tightly gripped the crook of Mr Robinson's arm as if afraid she'd drift to heaven if she let go. Who knows, maybe she would.

"I'm looking for my mom. Have you seen her?"

"You should not be here tonight, child," he said, snowflakes descending from his mouth as he spoke. "And neither should your mother. I tried to warn her, but the spirit she is with would not let me near."

"Where are they?" I said, desperately searching the floor again but seeing no sign. I felt a wet hand on my shoulder. Kyoko pointed towards the far end of the bar, near the door to the kitchen. There she was, or at least I thought it was her.

Mom was barely visible, surrounded by a large group of people, some in business suits, some in fancy gowns, others in sailor's uniforms. She wore an outfit I'd never seen on her before. A shiny green dress clung to her body, silver pearls looped around her thin neck and one of those feathered tiaras holding up her long black hair. The expression of pain that had been wearing her down this past year had vanished. She looked good, laughing, smiling, having the time of her life. It pissed me off. I stomped towards the bar, ready to ream her out.

The press of bodies around her was an impenetrable wall that I couldn't get past. I tried shoving a young couple out of the way. They shoved back so hard I fell on my butt. That's when I saw their faces—plastic skin, frozen smiles, hollow eyes. I'd never seen ghosts look like that before.

The two sailors next to Mom had the same fake faces, like Halloween masks welded to their heads. They leaned towards her intimately, whispering to her, their necks occasionally snapping back in laughter at her replies. No noise escaped their gaping mouths, at least none that I could hear.

Mom seemed to hear them just fine, judging by the way she blushed at the whispers in her ear.

"Don't have too much fun without me," said a man as he entered the club from the kitchen. He appeared to be of Chinese descent, although his flesh was powdery white. With his black tux and dark hair slicked with grease, it appeared as if he'd stepped straight out of a silent film. Only his too-red lips and the glasses of crimson wine in his hands said otherwise.

Paying me no attention, he moved towards my mother, the crowd parting for him like the Red Sea before Charlton Heston. I quickly slid through the gap behind him before the bodies could close back in. The plastic people pushed into me, slamming me against the bar. They squeezed me against the brass rail, taking the air out of my lungs, keeping me from screaming for help. I doubt help would have come anyway. The silence of the plastic faced people was even more apparent here, as if their lack of words covered the area with a thick blanket, muffling sound.

Only the voice of the singer penetrated, but her notes sounded distant, like they came from deep within a well.

I collapsed to the floor, sliding behind a barstool for safety. I managed to work my way from one stool to the next until I reached my mother. She accepted one of the drinks from the tux-man. Inside the glass sat a liquid as thick as oil, like no alcohol I knew. She sipped, making a face of delight. The tux-man leaned towards her and whispered something in her ear. Her eyes rolled back briefly, her face going pale, shiny, like the plastic expressions around her.

"Leave her alone!" I shouted. Leaning against the bar for strength, I kicked at his stool, throwing him backwards. The crowd parted around him as he staggered, giving me the space I needed to get up and reach my mother's side. "*Mah ma*, time to come home."

Her face cleared at the touch of my hand. Mom's dress shimmered, flashing between it and the truth of what she wore: an open bathrobe with a dirty nightgown underneath. "Charlotte? What are you doing here?" she said.

"That's a very good question," said the tux-man, straightening his cuffs and collar and glaring at me with cold eyes as he composed himself. No matter how alive the ghosts appeared through my goggles, their eyes always gave them away for what they were: dead, the orbs in their sockets holding an impenetrable blackness devoid of emotion.

I turned my back, placing myself between him and my mother. His stare chilled my neck like ice on my skin. I pleaded with her, trying to ignore him. "*Mah ma*, please come home. You promised me you'd stopped drinking. Jaiden's really upset again."

"Jaiden?" she said, confused. Then it dawned on her. "Oh,

my poor baby!" She put the drink down, revulsion mixing with horror at the sight of it in her hand. Her perfect hair dissolved into a dishevelled mess, full of frayed strands and split ends, while the constant pain she felt returned to her face, making me feel cruel for breaking the spell. She knew better than to drink, I thought angrily.

Mom had always quelled the spirit voices with a drop or two. On the day of the crash, she'd had too many glasses of wine when visiting a well-to-do client in West Vancouver. The cops said the alcohol probably slowed her reaction time when the truck in front of her came to a sudden stop in heavy traffic. She ploughed right under him, taking the roof off our old Chevy.

The drink slid back into her hand of its own accord, and her weary expression disappeared, replaced with longing. Before I could do anything, the tux-man came between us, his eyes boring into me. "Why don't you go home and deal with it yourself, Charlotte? This is no place for a child." His hand fell onto my wrist, his touch burning like dry ice. I yelped, tried to pull away, but his grip was too strong.

I searched desperately through the spirits for help but found none. Everyone had the same frozen plastic smiles. I realized then why I couldn't hear them. Mediums listen to souls. These things had none.

Tux-man tipped my mom's glass towards her mouth with his other hand. As she drank her green dress returned, glowing with synthetic sheen. Tux-man smiled, his lips growing redder as they curled with satisfaction.

I tried to fight, but his touch had iced over my entire body, leaving me stiff, defenceless. His lips appeared to grow larger as he leaned towards me. He nestled them by my ear and began to inhale, as if sucking soda through a straw. My vision blurred. My thoughts clouded. It was hard to remember why I was here. I felt the world drifting away, and I could do nothing to stop it.

That's when I knew he was *è guǐ*. A drinker of souls. Hopelessness welled up inside me.

Then I heard the song on stage change. The woman sang a soft solo, her voice taking on a Scottish accent:

Once I was a woman born,
'til he blackened my heart with scorn.
Until he blackened my heart with scorn.
Hunger now crawls upon my skin,
waiting for my death to begin.
Waiting for my death to begin . . .

The piano player accompanied her with a few keys, the clear notes penetrating the silence around me. All the dancers had stopped to look our way.

"Stay out of this, Nightingale," said the Tux-man, his eyes staring with malice towards the singer. I felt his grip weakening on my arm. The singer continued, the dancers joining their faint voices to hers.

Beware the washerwoman's son,
starvin' under the midnight sun.
Hungry for the midnight sun . . .

The man in the tux howled, his face suddenly crawling with black worms. They ate at his cheeks, and left puckered holes where his skin used to be. His scream sent the other ghosts racing away in fear. He let go of my arm before ripping off my goggles and backhanding me across the face. I went flying, hitting the ground with enough force to knock the wind out of me. The music fell silent.

Rolling over in pain, I coughed onto the floor. A dusty, dark floor. I turned back to the bar. Peeled paint and graffiti. An empty room. "No! No, no, no," I said, desperately searching for my goggles, which were nowhere to be seen. I searched the pub, the kitchen, I even went outside, but I could find no trace of them. No sign of the *è guǐ* or my mother.

Returning to the dance floor, I tried hard not to cry. Balling up my fists, I fought the impending meltdown. He had her. For the first time, I didn't know what to do.

A hand fell upon my shoulder. A wet hand. I glanced up, but saw nothing. Then my eyes drew towards the mirror. Next to my reflection floated Kyoko. The drowned woman smiled, beckoning me closer. Her wet hand guided me around the bar until I was right up against the mirror. Kyoko pointed to the corner of the room. I could see Mom in the reflection. She was being led into the kitchen by the man in the tux.

"Mom!" I cried, banging on the glass. She didn't hear me. The mirror showed the sepia tinged bar, the band's instruments on the stage, though no sign of the musicians or anyone else. "He's taken her all the way to the other side, hasn't he? You can show me, but can you take me there?" I asked Kyoko. She smiled and shoved me through.

My body felt like it was being sucked through a drain. I landed hard on the other side. Here everything was reversed, from the letters on the posters to the position of the front door. I was truly in the spirit world now, though all the ghosts had fled, even Kyoko. Walking to the kitchen door as quietly as I could, I slipped inside.

I scuttled into the middle of the kitchen and hid behind the counter, crouching next to an open garbage can. Every metal corner in here seemed sharp and rusted, bent and twisted. The open cupboards along the wall were bare except for a blood-stained rat sniffing around the top shelf, its dead eyes shining in the dark. The garbage can lid lay on the ground nearby, flies buzzing around the opening. It stank so badly that even the rat stayed away from it. Resting on the lip of the garbage can were my goggles. *Gross!* I grabbed them, wiping them off the best I could. I really did not want to put them on.

Luckily I didn't have to. I'd been pushed fully into the spirit world now, and I could see the *è guǐ*, plain as day. He hung over my mom in the corner of the kitchen, like a vulture waiting for his dinner to die. He no longer looked dapper. His body was stretched thin, his arms overly long, like the bent branches of a twisted tree. He had deeply recessed pits for eyes and cheeks pockmarked with yawning holes.

His bright red lips nestled by her head, puckered for a kiss. White light hissed out of her ear into his mouth. In the glow I saw images from her life, pictures that quickly flickered past like old celluloid film. He was sucking out her soul.

I picked up the garbage can lid at my feet and charged, screaming in a pitch so high I thought I might break glass. The lid slammed into him first, protecting me from his cold touch. I caught him off guard, knocking him to the ground. "We have to go, now!" I shouted at Mom, trying to ignore the sound of my voice, whiny with fear. I slapped her. No response.

My adrenalin-fuelled strength helped me dragged her back towards the door to the bar. The *è guǐ* rose in a dog-like crouch, howling, its mouth a gaping orifice that dripped with blood. I kicked over the stinking garbage can. Pulpy meat flowed towards him, making him scurry backwards.

The garbage moaned with human pain as it slid along the floor. I caught sight of a rotten arm, eyeballs darting around like they could still see, and hairy skin wrapped around a spine, slithering like a snake. I moved even faster. I dragged my mom back into the pub, and together we climbed through the mirror to the real world.

The howl followed us. I turned to see the *è guǐ* shambling his way towards the bar on the other side of the mirror. His hands scrabbled at our reflections. An icy chill passed through me. Its howl of frustration grew louder. It reached the mirror. A hand began to slide through. I grabbed a stool and smashed the glass, hoping to scatter his return to our world into a million pieces. If not, I'd given myself bad luck for nothing.

Without waiting to find out, I dragged Mom out the front door. I made all of five steps before tripping and falling on the hard cement outside. I looked into her blank face with worry. She had eyes only for the clear night sky above. *"Mah ma?"* I said, trying to control the choking emotion in my throat. Her face was pale and sweaty. I gave her a hard slap.

She blinked. "Please don't do that, Charlotte," she said, a smile appearing on her lips followed by tears in her eyes. "Oh, my little rice girl, I'm so sorry. Can you forgive me?"

Blinking back my own tears I nodded, laughing with relief. "Can we go home now? I really have to pee."

We staggered up the hill, neither of us daring to glance back at the abandoned pub behind us.

At home, Mom soothed Jaiden to sleep. His bottomless black eyes drifted closed, his pale face dissolving into a warm ball of light as he floated happily up to his corner of the room. My little brother, the wailing *guǐ*, was content, his cries quelled now that Mom was home.

I made sure my mother took her pain medication and tucked her into bed. I watched her until she was safely asleep, then stepped out and locked her door to prevent her from sleepwalking. I knew it would happen again, though. They would keep calling her out until one day only her *Hun* would go with them, leaving her pain-racked body behind.

After the car crash, they tried to fix her, but nobody could heal her sorrow or assuage her guilt. The doctors assured me she would recover, but I knew better. A medium should only hear the dead, not see them with bare eyes. I knew she was nearing her end.

I didn't know what Jaiden and I would do once she was gone, or if he would even stick around. Maybe Dad would finally come home. I didn't know. Until then I checked that all the doors were locked and crawled back under my nice thick comforter.

"Good night, Jai." My bobbing brother didn't answer. He was already fast asleep.

THINK TANK

Susan Pieters

Susan Pieters continues to surprise and delight us with stories in all genres, a different one for each issue. Aside from multiple appearances in Pulp Literature, her work is also featured in Tesseracts 20: Compostela *from Edge Publishing. She precedes 'Think Tank' with an apology to any persons, living or dead, who may think she's writing about them. She's not. Seriously she's not. She's just stealing the cast-off crumbs of anonymous lives to make her voodoo dolls, so that these events will never, ever happen.*

THINK TANK

It begins over pancakes.

Buttermilk pancakes are not a recommended twenty-second-century breakfast, but I've flown in for a visit with my daughter Carmen and the cast-iron skillet she found at the San Francisco RetroRecycle is just like the frying pan we used when she was a child. I tell Carmen the pancakes will soak up nutrients from the metal, and she needs the extra iron intake for the baby's sake.

I ladle batter onto the greased pan. Bubbles rise and collapse, but I know better than to turn the pancake over yet. I'm a patient woman. I wait for the holes to stay open after they pop, rather than caving in. At the edge of the pan, the butter has stopped sizzling and now browns darkly.

"It smells like Sunday mornings." My daughter Carmen moves her third-trimester belly sideways to get past me in the small kitchen.

"Or camping," I say, because she walks barefoot this morning, and it reminds me of how she always went around at the lake.

Carmen's husband Graham comes to the kitchen doorway

and looks at me. "Juanita?" He points to the stove. "Something's burning."

I offer him the ebony handle of the spatula. It has a wide paddle perfect for flipping. "You want to take over?"

Graham recoils then smiles like it's a joke. He backs out of the kitchen.

When my daughter leaves the room to set the table, I make a note of his reaction in my BaseLink. He's been at Infinity Insight for less than a year, and already, he's changed.

Graham drives us to see his workplace. It's across the Bay Bridge. Carmen is in the front seat of the electric floater car. We hover through the old freeway route to his office, passing the giant new Tesla2 building. Graham doesn't turn to gawk, since he commutes past here every day, but I give it an appreciative look. It looks like glossy origami. It dwarfs even the SpaceX high-rise, built to house the volunteer Martian colonists as they prepare to leave Earth for good.

He steers the car in front of a plain low building with no signage. "This is it. Infinity Insight."

The structure is so unremarkable, it's like the building doesn't exist. There's not even a street number on the door. Graham told Carmen that he's not sure who owns the building. The investors' names have been withheld, and the company's registered under a secured number. The person who hired my son-in-law is simply called Bob. He's the brother of somebody who owns so much internet real estate that no one knows his actual name.

"I can't show you everything, Juanita, but there's a section open to the public where you can go with Carmen."

"The wives' corner," my daughter jokes.

"Don't women work here too?"

"A few," Graham answers. "I tried to get Carmen to work here."

"Morning sickness didn't agree with my study of Derrida." Carmen shoulders her purse higher so it doesn't bang against her belly. "The arguments didn't make sense to me any more, in French or English."

"Hormones can affect the brain," Graham says.

"Or give you a different set of priorities," I say.

Carmen puts a hand on her bulging midsection. "It seemed pointless to debate whether a word has one meaning or an infinite number of meanings or no meaning, when all I wanted was to *use* the word to ask for a glass of water."

"But the theory is so integral to the usage, in the long term." Graham is cut off from saying more by the security guard, who checks his ID and ushers Graham to the left while we go to the right.

The room is decorated in early Americana, with a rustic log-cabin feel. Then I notice that the shelf with the decorative copper kettle has stained rings. I lift the pot and it's half full of water.

I finger the quilt on the couch. The thin worn fabric is carefully stitched in blocks. The lumpy batting inside is heavy with years of use and faded smells.

In the corner, a Ben Franklin stove is stocked with real logs, ready for a match, despite the building's temperature-controlled environment and the mild climate of the San Francisco Bay area.

I sit down next to Carmen and my head bumps the wall behind me. A dulcimer rattles and a string vibrates.

"Do you think you could play it, Mom?"

I shake my head. "It's not the same as a guitar."

"I've been trying to teach myself."

"Do you spend that much time here?"

"We meet for Book Club. All the women get together. There's one guy whose partner works here, but he doesn't join."

"What are you reading?"

She passes me a book off the shelf. There are a dozen low bookshelves surrounding the room.

"*War and Peace?*"

"It was good," she says, smiling at the cover like it's her friend.

"Did Graham read it?"

"He doesn't have time. He's been working on his Aristotle."

I make a face.

"In Greek, Mom. Infinity Insights said learning the original language was important. It's what the American forefathers did."

"You think George Washington studied Greek?"

"They all did. And Latin."

I flip through *War and Peace.* Somebody had pencilled notes in the margins. "What's really going on here, Carmen?"

"I told you, it's a think tank. Some guy with a lot of money to invest created this place. He wants the teams to come up with new ideas, just like the forefathers did."

She way she pronounces forefathers makes me close the book. "Do they study politics?"

"Among other things."

"Well, you've got the better end of the bargain, reading Tolstoy."

She smiles. "But now my list of baby names is turning Russian," she says. "Natasha, Mikhail, Nikolai ... "

I press a hand on her hard belly. "Girl or boy?"

Her eyelids drop in thought. "I think it's a boy," she says. "I hope so."

"Why?"

She blushes, and I regret asking.

I am packing to leave, my visit over, when Carmen stops me.

"Can I come home and stay with you in LA for the birth?"

Graham stands by her, not meeting my eye.

I close the lid to my suitcase. "But why?"

"I have a project due," he says.

"Now? Can't it wait? Aristotle's a few thousand years old, he's not going anywhere. This is the miracle of life you're about to experience."

"The baby won't notice." He looks at my suitcase and then out the window.

I study my daughter's face. It isn't the baby I'm concerned about.

I help Carmen pack. In the airport I make a note in my Base-Link and check that it recorded the way he said goodbye to her.

"I think you're jealous," Carmen says. She picks out a biography of Carl Jung from my shelf. I hope she appreciates that my books, unlike Graham's, are dusted and arranged in alphabetical order.

"Jealous?"

"Graham's got no training for his position. He was a software engineer when they scouted him. Yet he gets a peach of a job to do creative research. And you've got a PhD in psychology—"

"Ah, but I wouldn't have accepted his job." I put a glass of water by her usual chair and move the footstool so she can prop up her feet. Her ankles are swelling.

She settles herself. "The funny thing is, they seem to recruit people who don't have a classical education. Graham noticed that in the job interview. They kept asking for a *tabula rasa*. The ad was for fresh thinkers with no preconceived ideas."

"I wonder why."

Carmen picked up her glass. "Graham didn't."

Despite my best intentions, when Carmen went into labour, my grandmother hormones kicked in.

Being an over-involved mother is more forgivable among ethnic groups, and my Hispanic culture still venerates the role of nanny-grandmother. After the birth, in spite of the inner shrieking of my twenty-second-century education, I volunteered to be the full-time caretaker for Carmen and her son, Benjamin.

I rented a room near them in San Francisco, opting for a month-to-month lease that seemed flexible for my temporary situation. But it's nearly a year now, and Carmen thinks I should just buy a new place.

I adore my grandson Benjamin. He feels more my child in some ways than Carmen ever did. I didn't display pictures of Carmen when she was a child, but photos of Ben are on every surface of my life.

Graham is grateful. He missed Ben's birth by minutes. As a father, he's been behind ever since.

I clean the stove as Carmen spoon-feeds Ben. "But Graham will have the day off for Ben's birthday party, won't he? It's a Sunday."

Carmen was at the gym this morning and she's still in her sweaty Spandex. "But his final report is due." A drip of apple-sauce falls on her running shoes. She bends over to wipe it off. "Can we postpone the party?"

"Postpone it until when, Carmen? When Ben is two?"

Carmen doesn't answer.

Ben waves an animal cookie at me, and I drop the subject.

I stay late that night, waiting for Graham to come home. I heat him some leftovers as Carmen puts Ben to bed.

Graham thanks me for the food and then eats without talking.

I set the BaseLink to audio recording and slip it into my pocket before I carry in his dessert, a bowl of plain yogurt and fresh mango. "Do you realize you haven't taken a holiday since you began with Infinity Insights?"

"We questioned the concept of holidays just yesterday," he says, putting down his spoon. "It came up in our FreshLook meditation."

"Fresh look?"

He stammers. "I wasn't supposed to ... uh, it's a thing we do."

"It's okay, I won't tell Carmen."

He pretends he's doesn't care. "It's not a secret. It just a private practice we've developed."

"No worries."

"It's a process to question our assumptions."

"Seems like a good idea. Very Aristotelian."

"Exactly. Everyone does it, really. All cultures transform that way, at least all the powerful ones. It's the mark of people who create their own destiny."

"But does this mean you don't take holidays?"

"Ideally not. It disrupts the flow of regular routine." He dips his spoon in his yogurt, stirs everything around so it's evenly distributed. "Muscles build best with steady, regular use. Holidays only decrease strength. Seniors notice this when they stop exercising, like on cruise ships. They decline rapidly." His eyes furrow. "Are you a senior? I hope that doesn't offend you."

He clearly can't tell what I'm thinking. I'm not worried about my muscle tone, or being called a senior. "So you apply anecdotal stories to support your theories?"

"Yes. Stories are undervalued as sources of knowledge. Facts, or what people *call* facts, are really stories made out of numbers. And numbers themselves, well, they're just *names.* Group names."

"Group names."

"Like an age, for instance. I'm twenty-eight. That number labels me with a million other twenty-eight year old American males. But that's a misleading fact."

"You're not really twenty-eight?"

"I'm not *them.* I'm me. I'm a person. I'm *one.*"

The light outside is gone, the sun sinking into the offshore cloudbank in the Pacific, but he has the glow of a man watching a brilliant sunset. I can almost see why Carmen married him. "Where does this lead to?" I ask.

"It doesn't lead us, that's the point. We free our minds up, and we lead ourselves. We explore new options."

"Like our forefathers did?"

"Like *my* forefathers did." He states the fact so calmly it almost doesn't come across like a racist slur.

I watch him eat his yogurt. "You have Pilgrim ancestors?"

"No, Revolutionary War ancestors. People willing to die for their beliefs. People who made a personal sacrifice for freedom. They created the greatest country in the world three hundred and fifty years ago. But that original passion has been lost. Their fresh vision of the future has been missing —"

"Until now."

He doesn't blink. He takes me for an impotent old woman, a widow, a servant.

"Until now," he agrees.

"It's time to choose," I tell Carmen at the end of Ben's first birthday party. Ben learned to say *cake* today. He's quite bright. He shared both the word and the object freely with his guests, a collection of toddlers and mothers from Infinity Insight.

The only person missing was Graham.

"I can't be asked to make such a decision in one day." Carmen puts Ben to her breast to nurse him, his fingers sticky with green icing.

"It doesn't get any easier to wait. Thinking about it will prolong the agony."

"Procrastination by rationalization?" Carmen asks, getting Ben settled.

"Paralysis by analysis," I quote back. "I'm glad you haven't forgotten your upbringing."

"But what if Graham just needs more time? What if he really does quit his job next month like he promised?"

"History repeats itself, Carmen. You have two years of data to predict the future. Graham's getting more sucked into Infinity idealism than ever. He doesn't care about you except as a commodity. You're just an attribute of his own persona."

"Can't you let the experiment run a little longer?"

"I wouldn't even if I could. The League has voted to end the trials and shut down the Infinity lab."

"How many trials did they do?"

"I can't say. But you're not the only woman to lose her husband to this."

"But to leave him behind, to start the new colony without any adult males—"

"Is the only way to prevent regeneration of the culture. I'm sorry."

"What about Ben?"

"He's young. He'll never be raised with bias and egotism. He'll never look at you the way his father does, not seeing you."

Carmen looks down at Ben for some time, but she makes the right choice. She loves Ben too much not to.

"I'll make the arrangements." I pull out my BaseLink.

She sighs. "Can we bring some Tolstoy?"

"And more," I promise. "It's important to remember the past as it really was."

Ben is asleep at Carmen's breast. A drool of milk escapes his parted lips and his fingers lay loose, uncurled from their hold on his mother.

If only Graham had chosen better. If only he had understood the true nature of power and the deeper meaning of the research he had been tasked with. Even if he had only marvelled at the miracle of life his wife's body was able to produce, he might have been spared his fate and been allowed to come along with us.

"What will it be like on Mars?" Carmen asks, rising with Ben in her arms.

"It will be a long winter. But I promise you, it will be a bright spring."

THE WIND OF A TRAIN

Erin Kirsh

Erin Kirsh *is a writer and performer living in Vancouver. Her work has been published in* Arc Poetry Magazine, The Quilliad, Strange Days Books, *and* Geist, *where she took second place in their 10th Annual Literary Postcard Short Story Contest in 2014. Erin is the Executive Director of Vancouver Poetry House. With this gothic piece, Erin adds to the fine tradition of post-apocalyptic Canadian spec fic.*

The Wind of a Train

I have thirty minutes to get to the station. It doesn't really matter which station, anything on the line will work, only I'm not really sure where I've gotten to. I don't have the benefit of being from this city.

The Sinking was sudden. A lot of places, including the coastal city I lived in, shook then were swallowed by water. Those of us who were rescued got airlifted to other parts of the country, where, as it turns out, there's not enough room for all of us. I was an early recovery, I got here when people were feeling more hospitable. The city wasn't overrun then. Nobody wants to tell the survivors of a tragedy to fuck off until said survivors start inconveniencing them. So being a sort of pioneer of the good ship shitstorm, I have a shelter of sorts, but it'll be gone if I'm not back before midnight. If things are lawless in the day, at night they are competitively piratical. I didn't mean to be out so late, but this city's more or less unnavigable and it doesn't take much wandering to end up far from Woodbine or Coxwell or any of the four street names I've memorized. So I got lost, and now I've got two choices. Get back to the place where I'm somewhat comfortable and my stuff remains unpoached as of yet, or move in on someone else's territory and hope that the stuff I snatch is better than what I'd be giving up.

Twenty more minutes. I should've picked taller landmarks when I first set out. Picking buildings that may or may not be chain establishments was a lapse of judgment. I wish I could ask someone for directions to the subway, but they'd either be Settled and think I'm fucking up their society, or worse, they'd be Displaced. Settled would make me feel bubonic and burdensome, but a Displaced person would lead me in the wrong direction, steer me down some dark alley and mug me. Best case scenario, I mean. It could go way shittier than mugging, of course. I'm only saying mugging based on what I'd do if I were more desperate. The Sinking's been an adjustment for everyone, the Settled included, but they're not the ones getting lost on their way to the subway. Sure, they've got less space, their health care system is straining to accommodate even a fraction of the Displaced, and the after-midnight free-for-alls are new, but at least they didn't lose their everything.

I can already tell some of the late recoveries are lost causes. I'm not trying to sound unsympathetic, but it's right there: some folks just don't have the wherewithal for disaster. Before The Sinking they were probably optimists. Optimists are ill prepared for reality. Probably their high school teachers didn't force them to read dystopias. Probably their teachers were into Jane Austen or some shit like that. Me, I'm not feeling super-fucking-surprised that shit is currently as ugly as a half-eaten pigeon twitching on a sidewalk. I *am* feeling like maybe this city should have some fucking you-are-here signs, or some arrows pointing to major transit hubs.

Or maybe they do, and I'm just that far away from it all.

At least the Displaced won't be blocking the stations yet. The last train leaves at eleven twenty, and the Forces patrol till midnight. Maybe I could hole up in a subway station bathroom if I miss the train. Some of the stalls must have full coverage doors, the kind where you can't peek for shoes to see if someone's in there. Still, those are easily broken down. I bet scroungers pick people's packs off from subway bathrooms all the time. Maybe the janitors lock the external bathroom door after the last train. Maybe they take bribes. No. Too many variables to be a real contingency plan.

I need the green line, possibly blue. I should know this kind of information, but I haven't exactly had the clear mind of a monk lately. I shouldn't complain, though. I've heard through the Displaced network that other cities have started rejecting us. There're rumours that some places are shooting Displaced as they show up, but I think that's bullshit. People just like to get worked up.

I see cement stairs. Ha! With ten minutes to spare, too. I could have taken a stroll. There's nothing to mark that these stairs lead to a station, but late recoveries have been pulling off public signage so they can steal from early recoveries like me, so that's no reason to get discouraged.

The stairs are wide, slippery, and smell like piss. This definitely points to it being a subway station; those smelled like piss even before everything else did. There's no rail in the middle for people coming both in and out, though. I don't hear chiming, I don't hear chatter, I don't feel gusts from passing subways. Bad signs. The light above me is flickering. There's no reason for that. There are enough people desperate for employment that there shouldn't be a burnt-out bulb in this entire city. People'd work for next to nothing, but Settled folks aren't exactly scrambling to employ the Displaced. Fair enough. There've been a few stabbings over things my Nan would have called small potatoes. And there go the lights again.

Okay, it's definitely a subway station, and it's definitely empty. There's a yellow stripe on the far wall. Not my line. I think this one intersects with the green line at some point, but I don't know where. Not sure which side of the platform I'd have to be on to get there, either. The route maps have all been torn down. I've got eight minutes. Best bet is to get on the next train that comes and hope it takes me where I need to go. Maybe the green line East will come late. Maybe somebody's jumped onto the tracks; that'd slow it down. That's a real possibility. People have been pretty screwed up lately.

It's a little weird that nobody's in the ticket booths. The turnstile is clammy. The only lights are the flickering shitbulb near where the stairs let out and the low-watt ones spaced out over the tracks. The rest of the station is dark. Best to keep quiet and make myself small until I see headlights. It smells heavy in here — of body odour and something less recognizable.

Rumbling. Lights. The wind of a train. Safety can feel like strange things.

Something moved. Something low in the far right corner of the station. Maybe it's just some other scared early recovery, someone smart enough to keep to the dark. I shouldn't have stood in the lit part of the platform. The train is coming, I see its metal body. The smell is getting stronger. Something is moving low in the corner. There is a sound of wet lips, like a mouth smacking against some mushy thing. A hiss like a slow exhalation, a crunch of teeth trying tendon. The wind of the train strengthens. Something is moving low in the corner. The cars are all empty. The train doesn't even slow down.

FOR YOUR CONVENIENCE

F J Bergmann

F J Bergmann has manifested in Analog, Asimov's, Apex *and elsewhere in the alphabet, and functions, so to speak, as poetry editor of* Mobius: The Journal of Social Change *(mobiusmagazine.com). A* Catalogue of the Further Suns *(dystopian first-contact SF poems — don't say you weren't warned), won the 2017 Gold Line Press chapbook contest. 'For Your Convenience' is FJ's third story in* Pulp Literature. *It is every bit as irresistibly quirky and funny as 'Opening Doors' in Issue 6 and 'How to Lose a Week' in Issue 13, and we are happy to continue to provide you with this semi-regular FJB vending service.*

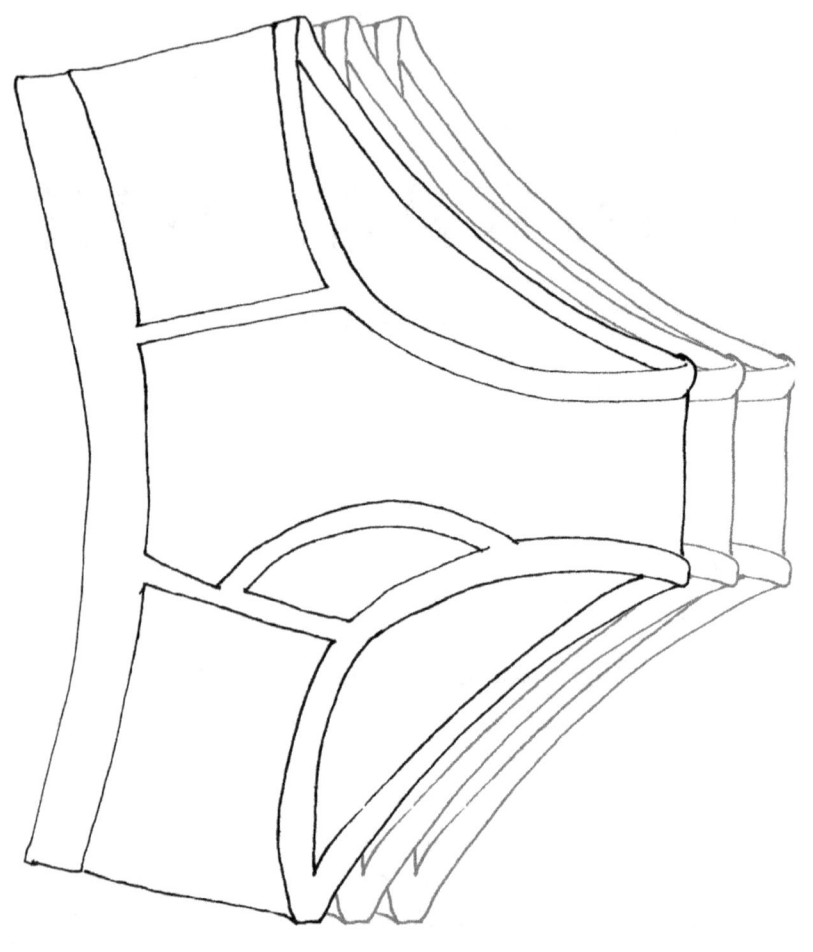

FOR YOUR CONVENIENCE

"I don't have all day, you know. Other people are waiting to use me. I'm *very* much in demand!" the vending machine's speaker blared as it towered over Larry.

The blinking of its red-lit buttons made it appear to be glowering, Larry thought. "You make the selections revolve too fast for me to get a good look," he complained. "And how do I know they'll fit? I can't even see a brand name!"

"Please insert appropriate change, or move aside as a courtesy to other customers."

"*What* other customers? I'm the only one here." Larry looked nervously into the impenetrable Stygian darkness outside the low barricade with its coin-operated turnstile.

"They'll be along, never fear. *Everyone* will be along, soon enough." Its tone was insufferably smug.

Larry swung a kick at it. "Ow, ow, ow." He hopped in a small circle on his other foot, grimacing.

"*I'm* reinforced with depleted uranium, ha-ha. *That*'ll teach you."

"*Fine.*" Larry's shoulders sagged. He eyed the rotating compartments hungrily. "H-1 . . . right? Men's briefs, three-pack, size medium." He grabbed a fistful of worn obols from the pocket of his cut-offs, counting them carefully before dropping them in the slot. "Seventeen … eighteen." He punched the buttons. A few clicking sounds emanated from the bowels of the machine. Larry waited, tense with anticipation. Nothing happened.

"Ten-percent damage surcharge."

Larry's howl of outrage was wordless but vehement.

"You kicked me, remember? I bruise easily."

Seething, Larry pulled out two more coins and dropped them in.

"Machine does not give change. All complaints must be filed with management within ten days."

"What a surprise," Larry muttered.

There was a thunk; the display revolved ponderously. A slithering sound, then a packet appeared in the dispenser opening. Larry grabbed it and ripped it open.

"AAAAUUUGGHH!"

The machine began looping a light, tinkling melody with the inane qualities of a perfect earworm.

"THESE ARE *WOMEN'S* UNDERPANTS! *BIKINI* WOMEN'S UNDERPANTS!"

The tinkling stopped. "They'll fit well enough. Soft, absorbent, pastel floral print. What could be finer?"

Larry spoke through gritted teeth. "Two years. Two fucking *years* I've been collecting coins. And you — you just — "

"And those obols. They just 'accidentally' fell off a few dead eyes, did they? Charon got a hole in his pocket?" the machine inquired coyly. The tinkling began again.

Larry turned his back and shoved his fists into *his* pockets.

The vending machine sighed heavily. "What in Hades do you want underwear *for*, anyway?"

Larry slowly blushed scarlet, or at least a gloomy eggplant shade. "It's my boyfriend. He ... um ... has a fetish for tighty-whities." There was a long pause. "And *you*—you—you've ruined everything! He also has a fetish for fauns and centaurs. How'm I going to compete with *that*?"

"The advice-vending machine is on the far side of the Styx."

"I need a refund, not advice! Either that, or the briefs. *Now.*"

"Machine does not give refunds. All complaints—"

Larry began shoving it, trying to rock it on its base, emitting infuriated grunts with each push.

"Do you want some help with that?" an interested contralto voice said, just as he collapsed against the machine, panting.

Larry whirled around. A large wolf stood just outside the enclosure. He began backing away slowly.

"Hi, I'm Lupa. This *is* the underwear vending machine, right?" She trotted nonchalantly under the turnstile.

"Good luck with that," Larry muttered despondently. "Um, I'm Larry." His forehead wrinkled. "Why does a wolf want underwear, anyway?"

The wolf snorted. "Use your eyes, boy."

She had pendulous teats—eight of them—hanging halfway to her knees. Or whatever those joints were called on wolves. Larry scratched his jaw. "Um. Yes, I can see where you might want to ... " His voice trailed off uncertainly.

She turned to face the machine. "What do you have in high-impact sports brassieres?"

The machine looked complacent. "Please insert appropriate change and make selection."

She gazed at the rapidly spinning display for a moment and turned to Larry. "Where does the speed adjust?"

He shrugged, and she turned back, looking the machine over carefully. "Plastic buttons are hard for me to manoeuvre with my teeth and claws. And I *just* don't *know* my own strength. When I tried to get directions to a friend's residence on the Plain of Jars from your fellow dispenser of advice, I ended up shattering most of its array, I'm afraid. And replacement parts are *so* hard to get down here." She sat on her haunches and yawned, showing long yellowish fangs.

The machine's display rotation slowed visibly, but it made an attempt at bluster. "Our bras are standard human: two cups each. No custom anything!"

She grinned, exposing her fangs again. "Then I expect to get a volume discount. I'll take four 28Bs, strapless, stretch cotton/ Lycra." She tilted her head to one side and pricked her ears. "Oh, and Romulus and Remus will be happy to lend a hand if there are any problems with your service. They're *such* good boys — so *big* and *strong*. And did I mention that Cerberus is a personal friend of mine?"

The vending machine sagged in defeat. "Maintenance access around the back: push the green oval buttons."

The wolf rose to all four feet gracefully and trotted around behind it. Larry followed.

"You can press the buttons," she murmured. "I wasn't kidding about the manoeuvrability part."

The machine opened easily. Once Lupa had made her selections, nudged them into a pile, and picked them up in her mouth, Larry quickly found the briefs he wanted. He shoved the bikini panties back into a random vacant slot and slammed the maintenance hatch closed.

"I have *nothing* to say to you," the machine said haughtily. Its lights blinked in a frenetic, random pattern and went out.

The wolf winked at him and loped off, leaping the enclosure wall in one bound. After a while, he heard distant howling. It sounded oddly joyous.

THE VANISHING DOT

Rina Piccolo

Rina Piccolo's *cartoons have appeared in numerous magazines including* The New Yorker, Barron's Business Magazine, Reader's Digest, Parade Magazine, *and more. Her co-authored daily comic* Rhymes With Orange *is syndicated in newspapers and websites worldwide. Her last appearance in* Pulp Literature *was with the graphic short story 'The Power of Centipedes' in Issue 7. You can find more from Rina at rinapiccolo.com. 'The Vanishing Dot' is a whimsical piece of nostalgia and wonder. We enjoyed this philosophical trip down memory lane, and we hope you will too.*

The VANISHING DOT
by Rina Piccolo

Like most people, I grew up watching television.

> What's GIVING tonight?

> nothin'.

My family owned the single requisite TV SET, planted in front of the sofa, dominating the living room like no other piece of furniture.

> Get outta the way! Can't see!

> How can you see anything through this dust?

That old-timey TV set was indeed a piece of furniture. Ours was made of wood, and stood on shapely, mahogany-coloured legs. It had panels, decorative moulding, even upholstery. You might say that the television of my childhood was the wired, vamped distant cousin of the pine bookcase, or China cabinet.

It had a smell: Sizzling electronics mingled with lemon-scented Pledge furniture polish.

nlike its cousins, however, the *TV SET* was connected to the world outside.

Inside its wooden exterior buzzed tubes, circuits, cords & coils —devices for delivering sights, sounds

...messages.

From the top of the set sprung rabbit ears.

I have to wonder why we call them "rabbit ears." The antennae were long, skinny sensory appendages —less like rabbit's ears, and more like the feelers of an insect.

There, too, was the SCREEN —

a mound of glass that curved outward as if to reach out to the viewer; not flat like today's screens, and not as sensitive, either. I remember touching it just to see the miniature lightening bolt that leapt to meet the tip of my finger, giving me a shock. (Okay, I guess the screen was, in its own way, "sensitive.")

The DIAL broke

...you gotta use these to change the channel...

When the TV set was switched ON it buzzed & warbled. If you touched its wooden parts you could feel it get warm. Seconds after the turn of the dial came the magic of HAPPY DAYS, THE MERRIE MELODIES, SESAME STREET.

But when the TV was turned off, there came through it another kind of magic.

...The Vanishing dot.

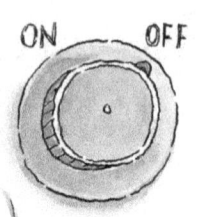

The dot appeared at the centre of the screen after the TV set had been turned off.

As broadcaster's voices faded and were silenced, the dot lingered on ...and on.

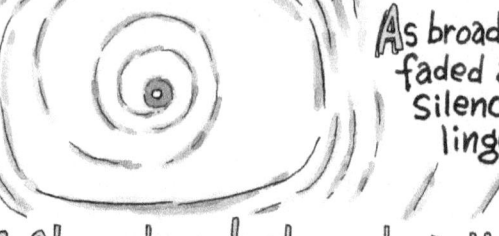

I stared and stared at the vanishing dot.

Was it a remnant of the screen's images—BUGS BUNNY, LUCY, BIG BIRD—collapsing further and further into a single speck on the dead, black screen?

If I peered in, would I see the images in miniature?

I did peer in.

I saw no tiny faces; no diminutive scenes.

The dot did not appear to be, as my nine year old self had imagined, a freakish window.

What I saw was glittery, blank light that writhed, and jittered.

White Noise.

No big deal.

The fact is, I might've gained renewed interest in the vanishing dot had I known that it was, and still is, a Kind of freakish window...

or, at the very least, an apperture.

Two decades after I peered into the vanishing dot, I learned something about white noise that made me revisit my childhood memory of it.

I learned that the white static we sometimes see, and hear, on old-timey TV sets, and radios, is radiation

—radiation from nearby electronics, the sun, and the very earth beneath our feet.

But some of it — a small percentage — is from the BIG BANG.

I gave that some thought. Seriously. Radiation—*light*—from the creation of the universe, the beginning of time, is reaching us...

through wooden TV sets that smell of lemon-scented Pledge?

Sounds like a fairy tale. How could it be true?

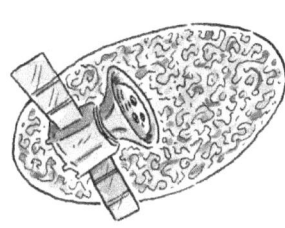

Physicists know it as CMB ~ Cosmic Microwave Background. It's defined as the cooled remnant of radiation from the Big Bang that fills the entire universe, and can be observed today with an average temperature of about 2.725 Kelvin (−270.425°C).

That's the sciency part. It's a little technical, but the magic it brings is the stuff of wonder —the kind of stuff that makes us question everything that may appear, at first glance, commonplace. It's the stuff that makes the smallest moments in our lives ~ like specks on a screen ~ worth peering into.

It's nice to have a memory from your childhood go from the mundane to the realm of the unusually beautiful.

what an upgrade!

Today I can say that back in the 1970s I watched GILLIGAN'S ISLAND, THE FLINTSTONES, and *light* — ancient light that began its journey across space to meet my nine year old eyes thirteen billion years before those eyes were born.

This channel gives nothing. Hand me the pliers!

Old-timey TV set, you rock.

end

ALLAIGNA'S SONG: ARIA

JM Landels

Allaigna's Song: Aria *is the second novel in the Allaigna's Song trilogy by equestrian swordswoman, artist, and editor JM Landels. The first book,* Overture, *was printed serially in issues 1 through 11 of* Pulp Literature, *and is now available in a single volume from Pulp Literature Press.*

$\mathscr{P}$REVIOUSLY IN ALLAIGNA'S SONG ...

Fleeing an unwanted betrothal and enraged by her family's lies concerning her parenthood, fourteen-year-old Allaigna has set off to find her true father. However, her quest is interrupted a mere three days in, when a chance encounter lands her in the illegal poaching encampment of her betrothed-to-be, Tiern Doniver. She is nearly recognized but escapes, thanks to new-found allies: the stable boy, Raddick, and the kennel master, Dog.

Fourteen years ago: Lauresa and her mother Irdaign have been reunited with the birth of Allaigna, but years of separation, anger, and memory loss leave unhealed wounds. Irdaign makes herself a part of the household under the assumed name of Angeley, while Lauresa struggles to forgive her and reconcile herself to her new role as mother. For reasons of her own, Irdaign clandestinely reunites Lauresa with her lover and Allaigna's father, Einavar, while Lauresa finds herself falling unexpectedly in love with her husband, Allenis.

Verse 6

The Bard's Bail

The sun was unseasonably bright and cheerful, I thought, given my mood.

I couldn't fathom what had possessed my self-appointed squire, Raddick—despite the eagle and a half worth of small coins I'd given him to complete his shopping errands—to attempt instead to steal a leg of cured mutton hanging from a butcher's stall. I learned the reason later: it was his pressing sense of obligation to me, wanting to save me a few coins and lessen the burden he made on my purse.

Of course he was already in the stocks by the time I'd spotted the commotion across the market square and pressed my laden way through the crowd. All of his purchases and his purse had been confiscated by the guard, and, after I bought Raddick's freedom, I had further negotiating to do to release his possessions. They were lighter by at least a third than they ought to be, but I had no way of proving it.

I loaded him up with my shopping as well, and sent him, shamefaced from my scolding, back to where Dog camped a league outside town. The reason we had separated in the first place was so I could buy new underclothes, and that task was still unfinished.

I set off, head down, grumbling at the inconvenience and cost of being liege to even one dim lad. I had only made fifty disgruntled paces when a large firm hand settled itself on my shoulder.

"Hold up a bit there, lad."

I came to a slow stop and gave an even slower quarter turn of the head, just enough to see my interlocutor. It was one of the city watch: not the thick-jawed clerk or the hoary veteran I'd dealt with for Raddick's release, but the one who'd been sitting at the back of the guardroom, whetting and oiling his sword.

Some rusty instinct began screaming at me to run, but I didn't pull back from the hand, which I felt would only tighten if I did. I simply stood, knees bent, weight on my toes to see how this new development would hinder me.

He walked to cross in front of me, that enormous hand never letting go of my shoulder as if in some strange madrigal. He held me at arm's length, studying both me and a sheet of parchment in his other hand.

"Nalen, is it?" he asked. It was the name I'd used to sign Raddick's release; but it was also the name, so foolishly close to my own, that I'd given at Doniver's camp. He must have felt the involuntary quiver that ran through me, for his grip tightened. "Ye'll need to come back to the guardhouse wi' me," he said, not unkindly.

My feet were glued to the cobbles, resisting the gentle pull on my shoulder.

"Naught to fear, lad," he encouraged. "A simple misunderstanding. Ye'll not be punished."

Fear warred with curiosity. What could that parchment say,

and what did it reveal about me? With practice borne of many sibling battles, I dropped down out of his grasp and twisted up again, snatching the parchment from his other hand as I hurtled off across the public square. The curiosity had hurt me, though. The twisting motion I'd used to reach the parchment had sent a twinge of pain through my knee, not to mention costing me a heartbeat of time. Sometimes I still wonder what difference that fraction of a second might have made.

As it was, I only just missed escaping down an alley as a drover backed his oxen into it. I tried anyway, hitting the cobbles with my already sore knee, and scrabbling like a lizard between the cart's moving wheels. I was almost home free when that large muscled hand clamped down on me again, this time on my ankle, and pulled me out like a load of washing against the washboard cobbles, not nearly so gentle this time around.

"I said, lad," he puffed, once he'd pulled me upright by the collar. "Yer master don't plan to punish ye. But make me run like that again and I might do it for him."

Thus I found myself in the holding room of the city watch, eyeing the window dubiously and waiting to find out my fate. I pulled the crumpled parchment from under my shirt. I'd had the presence of mind to stuff it there as the sergeant of the guard had retrieved me from under the cart. Crowding close to the window I turned my back to the door and smoothed the sheet out, peering at the words in the stingy light

. . . forsworn apprentice, Nalen by name, though he may give another . . .

Apprentice? Why was I being painted as a runaway tradesman's pupil? There followed a description I found most unflattering, particularly in regards to stature, but sadly accurate. How had anyone even seen my face long enough to note the mole below my right eye? And then I knew. The paper described my hair as black, but two days ago it had been a dirty blonde. I'd let the colouring charm fade, feeling it was safer to be my own colour once more, and indeed, my hair was now largely black. But Tiern Doniver had his own description, from the portrait he'd been given. Which meant he'd read the letters in my saddlebag and guessed my identity. I leaned against the wall, my knees no longer solid enough to support my weight on their own.

Would he send me home in disgrace? I wondered. Or, I shuddered, simply wed me here and now? He couldn't. He wouldn't. The grants of land and titles in my dowry would not apply if we were wed without the formal consent of the Duke. But what if he had consented already? Two days was time enough for a messenger to have gone and come from Teillai, bearing word of my appearance nearby, bearing permission to marry in return. That would certainly solve the Duke's errant daughter problem.

The words on the crumpled paper sprawled and squiggled as I imagined another notice:

Runaway daughter. Reward for capture. Lands, titles, hand in marriage . . .

I shook my head to clear it of these flights of painful fantasy. That was absurd. No matter how angry the Duke was, he wouldn't resort to such fairy tale theatre. I was, at least, fairly sure of that.

But he could quite easily have already granted permission to Doniver to marry me if he should find me. Doniver's own reward notice was real enough, and proof he knew my identity though he'd chosen not to reveal it. It would be embarrassing to have his bride-to-be picked up in the street like a criminal. Perhaps he was no longer interested in me as a marriage prospect, especially after the havoc I'd caused to his illicit pig operation. Did he seek to capture me for revenge? Or did he intend to gain some political leverage from my family? A queasy heaviness settled on me as I began to think what implicit demands could be made of my family, of how I had just handed more power to the person who least deserved it.

My miserable thoughts were interrupted as the guardsman who'd captured me opened the door and beckoned me forward. I stuffed the paper back under my shirt and followed him out of the tiny room.

"Yer apprentice?" he asked as we entered the main room.

A tall, thin man dressed in slightly crumpled velvet and silk stepped forward and grabbed me by the ear.

"That's the young rascal!"

The guardsman handed over to this stranger a bundle that looked like my possessions. The tall man tucked them under his arm while he shifted his pincer-like grip from my ear to my shoulder.

I took the opportunity to twist away.

"I'm no apprentice!" I shouted. "I've never seen this man in my life." My voice came out high and girly in the panic of the moment.

The large guard was blocking the outer doorway with his casual bulk; the clerk looked at me with only the mildest of interest, and the stranger, chuckling, closed the third side of the triangle around me.

"Tell them another one, lad. Your parents paid hard-won coin to settle you with me, and it's coin I'd rather spend than have to give back to their disappointed hands if I return without you. And think how sad they'll be when you come running home with your pockets and your head still empty, having squandered their hopes for naught."

His voice was musical, almost as hypnotic as Angeley's, though I sensed no Leisanmira magic beneath the words. I almost didn't notice that he'd grasped my upper arm in that firm grip again, and somehow silenced my protest.

He turned to the clerk. "The lad's a touch homesick, see. Though I have a suspicion it's not the charms of his mother's kitchen he misses, but those of the sweet barley-haired lass who kissed his cheek when I led him away."

He gave a broad wink, which somehow seemed directed at me as much as the clerk. I felt my cheeks burn with indignation, but a small part of me couldn't help but admire how he strung these lies out for his audience. In the end it was curiosity that bit me and let me walk out unprotesting. That, and the thought that it would be easier to cut and run from this single man out in the crowded streets than it would be to dodge him and the constables from within the guardhouse.

He tipped the guards and bade them a grateful farewell, his long-fingered hand still wrapped like a manacle around my bicep.

Once clear of the guardhouse door I wiggled a bit, testing his grasp. It was implacable. He pulled me in towards himself, curling his long frame down so his voice was in my ear.

"I don't know who you are really are, lad," he said in that low, musical voice, "but the one truth is I'll be paid well to bring you to Caer Doniver. Alive, yes. But no-one said anything about conscious. Now walk nicely, or I'll knock you cold and sling you over my shoulder like a sack of onions. Your choice."

"You've got the wrong person," I hissed at him.

"Oh la, I know that! But young Lord Doniver seems to want you to be a runaway apprentice, so who'll argue, eh?"

I could feel panic welling.

"Who are you?" I asked, hoping to distract him into loosening his grip.

"Why, don't tell me you don't recognize the lark of Aleran? Morran Rhoan at your service." He gave a mocking hint of a bow without loosening his grip a hair. "Though it's you who's at mine, isn't it?"

And then of course I did know him. A travelling minstrel, one who'd passed through Teillai many times when I was younger. He wasn't coiffed and kitted out as usual for those appearances in the great hall, but I should have recognized him nonetheless. He was one of Mother's favourites.

Should I reveal my identity? Appeal to him for help? But that would still hand me back to my family, and I wasn't feeling trusting. Instead I made a bluff.

"How much were you paid? I'll more than match it."

He laughed, loud and long enough to make the crowds we passed turn and look before resuming their business.

"I doubt that, young thing. Besides," he hefted my bundle of possessions, "I already seem to have all you're worth right here."

I opened my mouth to argue that my worth was more than my possessions … but that would lead to a discussion of who would pay for me.

I stumbled over the cobbles as I kept up with his long stride. The White Tooth of Caer Doniver loomed far too close. Desperate, I tried another tack.

"I do recognize you," I gasped. "I saw you sing in … " I couldn't say Teillai, or he might recognize me too. " … in Aleran, at the fair." I hoped it was true. Even the most popular court singers would not turn down the easy silver of market fairs.

I trolled my memory for one of those long-ago heard tunes my mother always requested, and sang, warbly, faintly, with lack of breath,

And rose in summertime
Blooms not so fair as thee
But flowers envy thy return
Lest thou come back to me . . .

He stopped and stared at me, his head turned at an odd angle.

"I spoke true without knowing it. You ought to be my apprentice. Where did you learn to sing like that?"

"My gran," I said, turning from his gaze. It was true enough, and farther than I wanted to go.

"What a shame Doniver seems set on having you. No, don't worry, lad." He didn't loosen his grip on my arm, but placed his other gently on my shoulder. "Tiern Doniver's tastes doesn't run to boys as far as I know. And he did ask for you unhurt. So I'm sure he means you no harm."

I was not nearly so sure.

Lauresa's Chorus

If her husband notices a chill between Lauresa and himself, he doesn't remark, perhaps attributing her distance to her increasing gravidity.

She keeps Allaigna close to her in the next two moons, seldom letting the child from her sight. Her daughter warms and thrives, basking in Lauresa's undivided attention. They spend time in her mother's garden, picking the season's first strawberries, their lips and aprons stained pink with this earliest foreshadowing of summer. They do puzzles and play cards together, Lauresa ever marvelling at the mathematically precise mind of her three-year-old daughter. They sing nursery rhymes, Lauresa's patchy memory pulling forth tattered threads and pieces that Angeley, when she overhears, joins in to weave together. The three generations of voice mingle to the delight of each and the enjoyment of anyone else within earshot.

Lauresa's joy is marred only by the foreboding urgency that causes her to glut herself on her daughter's presence, and enjoy her to the full while she can. It is a buffer against the wedge she knows will come between them: that other life harbouring in her belly. For now, she ignores it as best she can.

But ignoring can last only so long, and as the days approach midsummer, she knows this babe will be denied no longer. Shortly before the longest day of the year, Lauresa brings into the world a bawling, ruddy, nine-pound boy, changing her world once more, and her daughter's forever.

She is astounded, befuddled, and enraptured by the love she feels for this new baby: the one whose existence she tried to deny for the past months; the one who came, not from her lover, but from her husband; the usurper who arrived to take her precious daughter's place not just in her arms but in her inheritance as well.

She thought it was impossible to love another as fully, as unreservedly as she loves her first child. For how could her heart possibly hold any more? And yet she does. Despite the fact she doesn't want to, she loves him just as much. And because he is newborn and vulnerable, because his need is greatest, she appears to love him more.

She sees the pain in Allaigna's eyes and wants to take her in, hold her close in that sheltered world that once contained just the two of them; but her arms are full of Allenry. The constant strain of this double pull on her heart makes her irritable, prone to tears and to angry words. She snaps at her husband, her mother, and even, though she hates herself the moment it happens, her daughter.

Allaigna is angry too. Once a model child, it seems she has suddenly found a streak of venomous mischief within herself. A kiss delivered to her baby brother somehow makes him cry. The tiny hand so helpfully rocking his cradle moves faster and faster till the passenger slews about and wakes, while the grin on Allaigna's face stretches wider. The admonishments she receives from Lauresa and Angeley do little to stop such behaviour, and Lauresa suspects she knows why. No longer the centre of her own universe, lacking the attention she's had for the first three years of her life, Allaigna will attract attention from her mother and nurse any way she can, no matter the end result.

Lauresa tries to find time to spend with her daughter while the baby sleeps or is tended by Angeley. But she is so tired herself; what moments she finds are brief and hardly enough.

Allaigna is not the only one sensitive to the direction of maternal affection. Lauresa has heard that second babies are easier, less needy, than the first. But whenever she finds time for Allaigna, and Allaigna alone, Allenry awakes with uncanny promptness and demands to be fed, or changed, or simply carried. It is as if he is trying to make up for being ignored throughout the months of his gestation and is demanding his due now. And it is the guilt Lauresa feels for the months she ignored, resented, or even hated this baby that tips the balance. Fair enough, she thinks. Allaigna had me all to herself for three and a half years. She has been steeped in love. It will have to serve. She has her grandmother-nurse, and Allenry will have me. Not because it's what I want to choose. Because I have no choice.

Andreg is enamoured of his boy. If he suspects this is the only legitimate issue of their marriage, he still makes no mention of it. Perhaps it is simply that he has a male heir to secure the patrilineal succession common in Aerach. Lauresa seethes whenever she thinks of her adopted nation's barbaric laws, which will deny her daughter a title or holdings except by marriage. And yet, when she looks into her son's slate-blue newborn eyes, she wants the world for him. She wonders if she has become two people — Allainga's mother and Allenry's — and whether the two are reconcilable.

Angeley holds baby Allenry, rocking him while his eyes droop and then snap open, fighting sleep. The birthfeast has been held in the courtyard, the hall being too stuffy and dark in this beautiful summer weather. The sky is fading to teal, darkening overhead.

Lauresa leans over her mother's shoulder, passing a refilled goblet of wine to her.

"You shouldn't be playing the serving girl at your son's birthfeast, Lauresa," says Angeley.

"My castle. I can do what I want," Lauresa laughs. "And don't forget to address me as 'your Grace,'" she adds in a low voice.

"There's hardly anyone close enough to hear me, but fair point, your Grace."

Lauresa's glance passes over the wine-soaked lords and ladies lounging tipsily against what solid stone furnishings the lush garden provides. From where she stands they seem leagues away.

"Is Allaigna asleep?" asks Angeley.

Lauresa nods. "She was asking for you, but I told her a story and sang a lullaby, which eventually was enough."

"Better than enough. She needs you more than she needs me. Especially tonight, with all the fuss over this one."

Lauresa looks down at the sleepy baby in his grandmother's arms, at the eyes so desperately trying not to succumb to night.

"They seem to be getting darker, not lighter—his eyes, I mean."

"I think they'll be brown, like his father's," agrees Angeley.

"Why don't my babies have my eyes?" Lauresa half complains.

"They have plenty of other things of yours. Allaigna has your stubbornness, your sharp mind, your sense of justice. Though she'll look more like her father, I think she'll have something of your beauty as well."

"Her father's beauty would be enough," murmured Lauresa. "And what of Allenry? What will he have?"

"A sense of entitlement. Oh, and many other things as well." Angeley's voice had taken on its prophetic tones.

"And Allaigna? Won't she feel entitled as well?" Lauresa's heart cracks at the thought.

"No, she'll have to earn that, I'm afraid."

It surprises Lauresa that she needs to learn to nurse a baby all over again. So many things came back without effort: the automatic bouncing rock of her hips when she holds him; the comfortable way he fits wrapped against her chest in a shawl, scandalizing the notions of the other court ladies who have nurses or cradles to attend their babes while they tend the affairs of their keeps; the subtle cues he gives to let her know he is about to soil his swaddling, which gives her time to whisk him over a chamber pot or privy hole; the instinct that tells her he is about to wake from a nap. At all these she is so much more confident and proficient, so less worried by the trivial.

So why do her breasts not remember the sandpaper grating of a poor latch as he clamps her nipple between his gums and makes fruitless, clicking sucks? Again and again she breaks the latch, starts him over, and his round little face goes from turnip to beetroot, his mouth becomes a brick-shaped hole, and he clenches his fists like a prizefighter. At this point Allenis invariably wanders into the nursery and makes some proudly obtuse comment about his son's lungs, causing Lauresa to want to scream louder than Allenry.

He never spent so much time in the nursery when Allaigna was a babe, seethes Lauresa, tallying up the slights against her firstborn while resenting her husband's interest in the this one. *He is mine*, she wants to tell him. *Just because he is a boy does not mean he is any less mine.*

But there is still that other reason that makes him more Andreg's: the reason she won't mention anymore, even in her thoughts. It is not that she wants Andreg to love Allenry less — she simply wants him to love Allaigna as much. And if he did, she wonders, would she feel jealous and possessive of her daughter as well?

It is on such a morning of frustrated, interrupted nursing and ill-tempered musing that Angeley comes into the room, leading Allaigna by the hand.

"The painter is ready," her mother-cum-nurse announces.

Allenis scowls, though it was his idea to commission a portrait. Perhaps it is the fact the painter is one of Angeley's people that irks him so. Her husband and nurse can barely tolerate one another.

"He must wait till the maids have had time to dress my wife." He glances down at Allaigna in her worn tunic, rolled-up breeches and grubby bare feet. "And daughter," he adds with evident distaste.

Angeley curtsies, not meeting the Duke's eye, which is fortunate for both of them, given the ice Lauresa can feel coming from Angeley's averted gaze. "Your pardon, your Grace, but the tinctures are highly sensitive to the air. Once mixed they will not last long before losing vivacity. Every minute wasted will dull the final portrait."

And with every minute, Lauresa can see the Duke's good temper waning. Breaking the latch that has only just succeeded, Lauresa stands, tucking her wet breast back into her bodice.

"Husband," she says, handing him the objecting child. "If you would be so kind as to take your son"—there is ever so slight an emphasis on the last word—"we ladies will clean up and meet you in the hall." She leans across the bundle of baby and kisses Allenis on the lips, a feather-light touch with a hint of promise.

His shoulders relax, and he smiles and takes her hand with his free one, kissing the fingers as he takes his leave, unperturbed by the increasing, fussy squalls from the bundle in his arm.

Lauresa's tense back releases as well, and she lets out a long breath. Whatever her failings as a mother and wife, she has not lost her charm.

"Come, my darling," she says to Allaigna. "Let's wash our faces, brush our hair, and put on our best smiles for the painter."

VERSE 7
DONIVER

It was my feet that gave me away. They had fallen of their own accord into a trotting double-time rhythm to Morran Rhoan's long strides, but as we passed under the rusty, half-lowered portcullis of the keep, they faltered. Rhoan's grip had been loosening on my arm as we progressed, but the hesitation in my legs made those fingers tighten, noose-like, on my upper arm again. I looked over my shoulder as my last chance to escape disappeared behind me.

I wondered whether I'd be taken to a dungeon or a high tower, clapped in chains or locked behind doors, but it turned out to be none of these. Morran Rhoan led me to a small office adjoining the solar, and without pausing to demand audience, strode in.

Tiern Doniver was seated at a counting table, and Yannick—the Barrel—stood at his shoulder, both of them engrossed in documents spread across the table. Yannick looked up first, a large unfriendly grin spreading through the black bristles of his beard.

"It's the little troublemaker," he rumbled, causing Doniver to glance up as well. A sharp, equally unwelcoming smile grew on his face.

"Bring him here," he commanded Rhoan, beckoning with a roll of sheepskin.

The bard had to tug harder at my rapidly numbing arm, for my feet had glued themselves to the floor. He jerked, and I stumbled forward, fetching up against the table, scattering rolls of parchment in the process. Doniver seemed not to care about his papers. He reached across and grasped my chin in his cold fingers, peering at my face, nodding.

"Yes, that's the one."

He let go of my chin, reached beneath the table and procured a neatly tied bag that dropped on the table with a heavy clink. If those were eagles, there must have been fifty in there: a small fortune.

"Thank you, Rhoan."

The singer reached over my shoulder to pick up the sack. In its place he left the bundle of my possessions. As he left the room I glanced back at him, and he at me. I put a hand on top of the bundle.

"You too, Yannick."

The Barrel looked surprised. "Are you sure?" he rumbled.

"I think I can defend myself from a ragged, unarmed boy," was Doniver's mild reply. He snatched the bundle from under my hand and unrolled it like a card-sharp fanning out his trumps. From the meagre pile he removed my hunting knife and the curved dagger, placing them beneath the table, out of sight.

"Yes, Yannick, I'm sure," he snapped when the Barrel had still made no move to go.

Finally the immense man left to the sound of tapping from Doniver's fingers.

"So, Allaigna," he began. I didn't blink, certain as I had been already that he'd divined my identity. "Your family must be worried half to death about you. I was just composing a letter to tell them you were in such a hurry to be wed that you ran here to my arms rather than wait for the tedious betrothal to end."

He was lying. I didn't know how I knew, but I realized with

certainty he had no intention of writing any letter ... yet. It was both a relief and a worry. Any threat he might make then—to send me home, to formalize the betrothal—was an empty bluff I could ignore. The worry, though, was what he did want from me, and why it was worth as many eagles as he'd just paid Morran Rhoan.

What value could I have to him? As a hostage I had none if no-one knew I was here. As a bride my value was in alliance, which was also worthless if I was anonymous. And if he wanted from me what could be had from any dairymaid or courtesan? Well, I was hardly worth fifty eagles in that regard.

"But come," he said, standing. "You are tired and hungry, no doubt. You'll pardon me if I don't take your arm, dressed as you are." He flashed a quick and almost charming smile.

The elaborate courtesy was an utter contrast to the beastly fury I'd seen on his face when he'd struck and nearly choked me two days ago. I tried not to let it disarm me. But I was hungry.

He motioned to the door.

"Don't run," he murmured as he led me out of the counting room and across the solar. "You wouldn't get farther than ten yards."

It was likely true. Morran Rhoan had led me past at least a dozen men-at-arms in the courtyard and within the castle, and Doniver could alert them all with a word.

There was a small dining room across the solar from the office, and it was here, again with grandest courtesy, he offered me a seat. When the serving maid he called had come and gone, leaving bread, cheese, cold meat, and curious glances, he poured us each a cup of wine.

"Your health, my dear." He raised his goblet.

When I didn't respond in kind, he looked hurt.

"Come now, I hardly brought you here to poison you."

I had yet to open my mouth in his presence, but drinking seemed preferable to explaining that I didn't tolerate wine well. I would not show him even that weakness, so I took a sip, held it in my mouth, and swallowed slowly. At least it was well watered.

At his insistence, I helped myself to bread and cheese, and waited, still silent, for him to explain himself.

"Make no mistake," he said. "I am extraordinarily angry still for the mischief you caused. Though had I known who you were ... " He paused, reached out, and tried to touch the fading bruise on the side of my face. "You must accept my apologies for striking you."

Must I? I dodged his touch.

His look of sincerity didn't sway me. It was fine to strike boys, by his reckoning, but not girls? Or just not highborn girls he might want to marry?

"Nor do I know the true reason you left your home." He left a pause for me to enlighten him, but it would take more bait than that to draw me out.

"But I suspect that if you'd left with your parents' blessing you would not be dressed as a boy and travelling on your own. Though you're not really on your own now, are you? How are my kennel master and stablehand?"

I kept silent still.

He shrugged. "Whatever your reasons, I imagine your identity has a price. What, I wonder, would you do to keep it to yourself?"

Anything, I thought. *Everything.* But no, there were many, many things I would not do. I would buy his silence, but I would drive a hard bargain.

My voice was hoarse, as if it had been silent for weeks, not minutes. "You obviously have some price in mind." It was a childlike whisper, not the wry adult sound I'd hoped for.

"Ah, the little bird can indeed sing."

I flinched. Edris used to call me that. It was wrong, fouled, coming from his lips. But the thought of the strong and stubborn swordsmith lent me a spine of iron. I thought too of Garæthiel, with her smooth and easy tongue, her courtly, graceful manner that oiled the subtle wheels of intrigue. I would be both, I thought: sweet and subtle, with a centre of steel.

I gave a slight smile, inclining my head, my silence soft and inviting this time, waiting for him to take the first step into it.

"Well, sweet bird. Negotiation must begin with a certain level of trust, must it not? To start with, I'd like a tale. Not just any tale. I'd like to know why you're here."

I lifted my eyebrows. "Did you not order me brought here, my lord?"

The 'lord' was a gift: a free offering to sweeten the mood. As Andreg's daughter, I outranked him. In fact, I could command fealty in Andreg's name should I choose to play that card. He knew that too, but accepted my gift with either grace or arrogance. My reading of his expression wasn't profound enough to tell which.

"Are we going to dance this out then, Allaigna? Very well, let me rephrase. What were you doing in Doniver? And before you reply 'shopping', you should know I mean in Doniver in the company of my stablehand. With whom you seem to have been in collusion when you admitted yourself to my encampment under false pretences and proceeded to ruin what would have been a very profitable venture, not to mention a lot of entertainment for the masses."

"That's a very long question, Sir Doniver." I took a minute sip of wine to compose my answer. "I was indeed shopping. To replace the things I lost when my saddlebags were stolen. And I believe you still have them ... my lord?" I shot him a look.

It was his turn to raise eyebrows.

"For how else did you know my identity?" I continued, throwing his phrasing back at him. "And before you claim to have recognized me from portraits and our few meetings, consider that you hardly saw me long enough, or in full daylight.

"And since, as you say, negotiations are based on trust, I trust you to return those effects in full."

He inclined his head but said nothing. I took that to mean assent. Point to me.

I took another deep breath. "As to what I was doing at that camp, I had come across evidence of poaching in the common woods, which, as you know are part of my father's demesne. I was investigating."

His look chilled somewhat, but his smile stayed in place. "And finding it was I who has a legal right as liege regent of Doniver to hunt these lands, you must have decided to leave well enough alone, no?"

Instead of fixing a false smile to my face to match his, I left my features as mild and dispassionate as possible.

"Perhaps you have lost track of your calendar? It is, I believe, still the month of Ranis, and as you must be aware, taking of game is prohibited for another five clearmoons. Even for those of us with rights of the hunt."

"*Killing* is prohibited, indeed. But all those piglets were rescued.

It has been a hard winter, and many sows have not fared well. We cull their litters, lessening the burden on the sows and ensuring the ones we take are raised and fed."

"And yet your humane culling process seems to leave wounded sows behind."

He shook his head. "Only in the most unfortunate circumstances. Our hounds draw out the sow and a few of our men keep her away while others take half the piglets. The sow that you found — and thank you so much, by the way, for skinning, gutting and bringing her to us — was intractable. My men had no choice but to kill her, which is why we took all, not just some, of the marcassins."

It was almost plausible, and he seemed so regretful I just about forgot my outrage. But the lie was there.

They didn't kill her. They left her wounded and mad with pain. But surely he knew that — otherwise it would have been his men, not me, who brought the carcass in. I decided to hold that in reserve in case I needed it later.

"In that case, my father will be relieved and grateful to know you take such care with the management of the wildlife in these forests. I will be sure to commend you to him should I happen to see him soon."

And there it was, my threat to counter his own. Send me back to my family, or alert them to my whereabouts, and I would spill his secret. "After all, animal baiting is illegal all year round."

My small thrill of triumph was undercut by fear. It was a high-stakes game I played. I had just let him know that to send me back home or even admit my presence here to my family was to let them know of his highly questionable activities in the woods. I had increased his incentive to simply dispose of me.

My safety depended on my having read him aright: that there was something he wanted from me that would ensure I'd be kept alive. I hoped only it was not what he had already been promised.

"It would seem, my dear," he said, eyes hard now, "that you have no wish to be reunited with your family."

I swallowed. Had I overplayed my hand? "I am in no hurry," I responded as calmly as I could, though in fact, what I wanted now more than anything was my mother's and grandmother's arms around me.

"They are looking, you know. And are offering to pay, not just for your safe return, but merely for word of you. Oh, not to worry," he added with a patronizing pat on my sleeve. "Word hasn't gone out to the commons. Only to the noble and friendly families. The fear of ransom demands prevents them from making your absence known to the rabble."

I was not reassured.

"So you might wonder," he asked, "why have I not already sent word?"

I didn't respond.

He took a sudden change of tack. "Why did you run away? Some secret beau you're planning to meet? It can't be Raddick!" He laughed. "No? The life of a duke's daughter is just insupportably hard, and you thought grubbing in the woods would be easier?"

He reached for the flagon and refilled his goblet without offering to refill mine. "Or were you jilted, perhaps? Broken-hearted by some young swain? That's not it either. The prospect of marrying me, then?"

My face must have given something away.

"Aha," he said. "Am I so repulsive? Sorry to hear it."

179

He didn't look sorry, but I responded anyway. "Not you. Anyone."

"You prefer maids, is that it?

I felt my skin fill with hot blood. "No—"

"So you do have a swain somewhere."

"No!"

"It's all right," he continued, ignoring my interruption. "I would certainly allow you your lovers, providing you allowed me mine."

My face, my whole being, was burning with shame, embarrassment, and outrage. I didn't want this knowledge, or to be having this conversation. But my outrage was causing me to lose what control I had over this conversation. With a deep breath I mustered myself.

"Sir," I spoke between my teeth, "I'm no sighing romantic with thoughts of marrying for love. I simply have no wish to be a pawn—or even a queen—on the chessboard of our nations."

"Despite your father's reliance on you as such?"

"Because of it." I held up a hand. "Before you jump to conclusions, I bear the Duke no malice. I simply refuse to accord him the right of disposing of me to suit his aims."

"You don't believe closer ties to Doniver would benefit us all: Teillai, Doniver, Aerach … and you and me?"

"Perhaps they may. But they will have to be bought with other coin than me."

"Your sire has the right, by the laws of the land you were spouting at me a few minutes past—"

"Then those laws, in this respect, are wrong."

"And you intend to challenge them by removing yourself from the equation?"

"I intend to remove myself to somewhere the laws are more just."

He was looking at me differently now, the smug superior arch to his brow replaced with what seemed to be genuine interest. With his face so changed I could almost see him as attractive. "And what will you do in Brandishear, since that must be where you're heading?"

I started back in my seat, my mind spinning frantically. I'd said too much, been lulled by this conversation of almost-equals.

"Brandishear is not the only principality that keeps the old ways."

"It's a long way to Elalantar on that bony nag of yours … "

I blinked slowly, letting him follow his own conclusions.

" … and all the ports are in the other direction. No. It seems to me you're heading to the Valnirata borders."

I held on to my blank look, puzzled though I was at the direction this was going.

"You spin a pretty tale, little bird." He shook his head, chestnut hair swinging in the sunlight.

"Allenis Andreg is too careful of all things to allow something as obvious as a daughter to slip through his fingers."

Does he even know? I thought. I had been gone but five days, and he was in Aleran when I left. Had Mother sent word to him? I had no idea. And if he knew, would he even care? Still, Doniver was right—his pride alone would not want me to be here now.

Doniver's voice burbled over top of my musing. I only half paid attention to it.

"The more interesting question," that voice interrupted my thoughts again, "is why he'd use his daughter as envoy to the Ilvani."

I started, blindsided by the question, which had come from

nowhere in my horizons. It must have made me look like he'd hit upon my secret.

"Obviously not an official ambassador," he continued, "or you wouldn't be stealing my stablehand to serve as your retinue." He reached inside his doublet and pulled out a flattened roll of parchment.

My eyes widened and I nearly laughed as I recognized it.

"So what message could be so secret only a member of the family, dressed in rags and alone, could be trusted to deliver it?"

My mind was racing furiously, clicking over and over like a waterwheel in a torrent. He was no skilled interrogator, I realized. Instead, he was so proud of his own erroneous deductions he needed to boast of them. He had laid out the whole story he'd constructed for me, and now waited for me to step into the shoes he'd cobbled to size.

Should I do it, I wondered. He was so caught in his web of clever deductions that the simple truth—that I was a common runaway, angry at my parents, in search of my own history and destiny like any other truant child—would be unbelievable to him. But following his line of thought could be hazardous, and difficult. Could I even pull it off?

The paper he held was one of the copies I'd made of Ilvani missives from the Teillai archives, dating back to my grandfather's wars. I'd brought them along to study the language: if my real father was of that race, knowledge of his tongue might prove necessary. The fact Doniver took them for current missives meant he'd either not shown them to anyone else or he had no-one close to him who could translate them.

I maintained my passive silence as he unrolled the parchment. "But surely your father has many messengers. Why you?"

He peered at me over the paper. "He couldn't possibly be offering you as hostage. What could require that huge a surety?"

I raised an eyebrow. I didn't want him going down that track—he might begin to consider ransoming me himself. Time to speak.

"Espaegh dhi Yllvaeni?" I asked. *Do you speak Ilvani?*

His blank look was my answer, and my bargaining chip.

§

Allaigna's Song: Aria *will continue in* Pulp Literature I*ssue 17, Winter 2018. The prequel,* Allaigna's Song: Overture *is available through Pulp Literature Press and Amazon.com*

Allaigna's Song
Overture

JM Landels

THE ARTISTS

Akem
Cover artist, 'Seabus'
Akem forgot she was an illustrator and writer for a few years and is making up for lost time. Her first picture book, a myth about before we were born, is in progress. In the meantime, check out www.akemiart.ca for a series of fantasy illustrations and social media whereabouts.

Rina Piccolo,
Illustrator, 'The Vanishing Dot'
Rina Piccolo's cartoons have appeared in numerous magazines including *The New Yorker, Barron's Business Magazine, Reader's Digest, Parade Magazine,* and more. Her co-authored daily comic Rhymes With Orange is syndicated in newspapers and websites worldwide. Rina lives in Toronto, where she was born and raised. Her syndicated daily comic strip *Tina's Groove* ran from 2002 to 2017. Rina is also the co-author of the book *Quirky Quarks: A Cartoon Guide to the Fascinating Realm of Physics* (Springer, 2016). You can find more from Rina at rinapiccolo.com.

Mel Anastasiou
In-house illustrator
Mel Anastasiou loves drawing for *Pulp Literature* because she loves the stories she illustrates. She draws in black and white, working from imagination and inspired by details from Renaissance compositions. You can find more illustrations, as well as writing tips and news about her books and novellas at melanastasiou.wordpress.com.

JM Landels
Illustrator, *Allaigna's Song: Aria*
JM Landels studied at the Cartoon Centre in London, UK, under David Lloyd (*V for Vendetta*) and Dougie Braithwaite (*Punisher*). Although she is a perennial doodler, she put down her pencils and brushes after giving birth to three children, but rapidly dusted them off when she realized *Pulp Literature* was going to be an illustrated magazine. She blogs sporadically at jmlandels.stiffbunnies.com.

Thirty Days Towards
An Extraordinary Volume

THE WRITER'S
BOON COMPANION

Mel Anastasiou

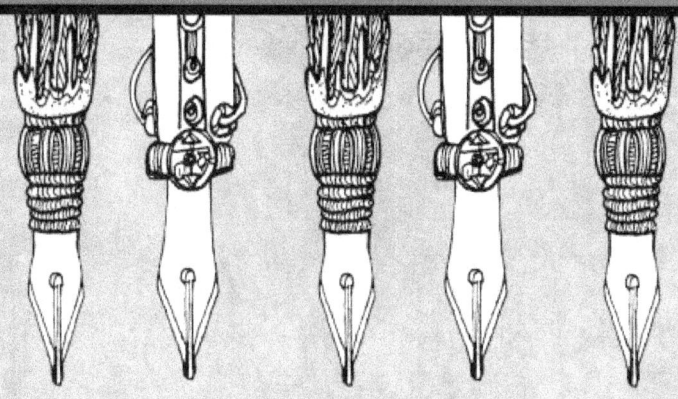

CONTESTS

Pulp Literature runs four annual contests for poetry, flash fiction, and short stories. For contest guidelines, prizes and entry fees, see our website, pulpliterature.com/contests.

The Bumblebee Flash Fiction Contest
Contest opens: 1 January 2018
Deadline: 15 February 2018
Winner notified: 15 March 2018
Winner published in: Issue 19, Summer 2018

Prize: $300 The Magpie Award for Poetry
Contest opens: 1 March 2018
Deadline: 15 April 2018
Winner notified: 15 May 2018
Winner published in: Issue 20, Autumn 2018
Prize: $500

The Hummingbird Flash Fiction Prize
Contest opens: 1 May 2018
Deadline: 15 June 2018
Winner notified: 15 July 2018
Winner published in: Issue 21, Winter 2019
Prize: $300

The Raven Short Story Contest
Contest opens: 1 September 2018
Deadline: 15 October 2018
Winner notified: 15 November 2018
Winner published in: Issue 22, Spring 2019
Prize: $300

MARKETPLACE

Books

Allaigna's Song: Overture *by JM Landels.* Music, magic, and the shaping of a hero.
pulpliterature.com/allaignas-song-overture

Paperboy: A Dysfunctional Novel *by Bob Thurber.* Photography by Vincent Louis Carrella.
shantiarts.co/uploads/files/thurber_paperboy.html

Stella Ryman and the Fairmount Manor Mysteries *by Mel Anastasiou.* Trapped in a down-at-the-heels care home. You'd be cranky too.
pulpliterature.com/stella-ryman-and-the-fairmount-manor-mysteries

The Writer's Boon Companion *by Mel Anastasiou.* Thirty Days Towards an Extraordinary Volume.
pulpliterature.com/subscribe/the-bookstore

Dear Geist...

I have been writing and rewriting a creative non-fiction story for about a year. How do I know when the story is ready to send out?

—*Teetering, Gimli MB*

Which is correct, 4:00, four o'clock or 1600 h?
—Floria, Windsor ON

Dear Geist,
In my fiction writing workshop, one person said I should write a lot more about the dad character. Another person said that the dad character is superfluous and I should delete him. Both of these writers are very astute. Help!

—Dave, Red Deer AB

Advice for the Lit-Lorn

Are you a writer?
Do you have a writing question, conundrum, dispute, dilemma, quandary or pickle?

Geist offers free professional advice to writers of fiction, non-fiction and everything in between, straight from Mary Schendlinger (Senior Editor of *Geist* for 25 years) and *Geist* editorial staff.

Send your question to advice@geist.com.

We will reply to all answerable questions, whether or not we post them.

geist.com/lit-lorn

GEIST
FACT · FICTION · NORTH of AMERICA

Bookstores

Book Warehouse
632 Broadway W,
Vancouver, BC
V5Z 1G1
(604) 872-5711
bookwarehouse.ca

The Comicshop
3518 W 4th Ave,
Vancouver, BC
V6R 1N8
(604) 738-8122
thecomicshop.ca

**Myth Hawker
Travelling Bookstore**
Canadian authors • Canadian
content • small and independent press
mythhawker.ca

Phoenix On Bowen
992 Dorman Rd,
Bowen Island, BC
V0N 1G0
(604) 947-2793

People's Co-op Bookstore
1391 Commercial Dr,
Vancouver, BC
V5L 3X5
(604) 253-6442
coopbks@telus.net

Regent Bookstore
5800 University Blvd,
Vancouver, BC
V6T 2E4
(604) 228-1820
regentbookstore.com

**Village Books &
Coffeeshop**
130-12031 First Ave,
Richmond, BC
V7E 3M1
(604) 272-6601
villagebooks@shaw.ca

**White Dwarf/Dead Write
Books**
3715 West 10th Ave,
Vancouver, BC
V6R 2G5
(604) 228-8223
whitedwarf@deadwrite.com

CONFERENCES & EVENTS

CONFERENCES & EVENTS

Surrey International Writers' Conference
19–22 October 2017
Surrey, BC
siwc.ca

Creative Ink Festival
for writers, artists & readers
18-20 May 2018,
Burnaby, BC
Creativeinkfestival.com

MAGAZINES

Geist
Ideas + Culture • Made in Canada
geist.com

Mystery Weekly Magazine
The cutting edge of short mystery fiction
www.mysteryweekly.com

Neo-opsis
Canadian magazine of science fiction, based in Victoria, BC
neo-opsis.ca

Polar Borealis
Paying market for new Canadian SF&F writers & artists
polarborealis.ca

Room Magazine
Literature, Art, and Feminism since 1975
roommagazine.com

𝒫RINTING & PUBLISHING
First Choice Books / Victoria Bindery
Book Printing & Binding
Graphic Design · eBooks
Marketing Materials
1-800-957-0561
firstchoicebooks.ca

Wesbrook Bay Publishing
Beverley Boissery, author and publisher
wesbrookbaybooks.com

POLAR BOREALIS

Magazine of Canadian Speculative Fiction
(Issue #4 – July/August 2017)

FICTION / POETRY

1st Prize: $1000 + publication (*in each genre*)
2nd Prize: $250 + publication (*in each genre*)
Judges: Sigal Samuel (*fiction*)
& Jónína Kirton (*poetry*)
Deadline: July 15, 2017

COVER ART

1st Prize: $500 + publication on a cover of *Room*
Deadline: November 30, 2017

SHORT FORMS

1st Prize: $500 + publication (*two awarded*)
Deadline: January 15, 2018

CREATIVE NON-FICTION

1st Prize: $500 + publication
2nd Prize: $250 + publication
Deadline: March 8, 2018

• •

Entry Fee: $35 CAD ($42 US for International
entries). Entry includes a one-year subscription to
Room. Additional entries $7. For more information,
visit www.roommagazine.com/contests.

ℬECOME A PATRON OF PULP LITERATURE!

By supporting *Pulp Literature* on Patreon with $2 or more per month, you will be laying the foundation for a secure future for the magazine, as well as ensuring you will never miss an issue! Your subscription includes four big issues of short stories, novellas, poetry, comics and novel excerpts delivered to your door or electronic mailbox each year.

Find us at patreon.com/pulplit
If you prefer to subscribe through our website go to pulpliterature. com/subscribe.

Or you can send a cheque with the form below to:
Subscriptions
Pulp Literature Press
8540 Elsmore Road, Richmond, BC V7C 2A1, Canada

....

Don't miss an issue!

- ❑ **Send me 2 years (8 issues) at the special rate of $80** (save $40)*
- ❑ **Send me 1 year (4 issues) for $50** (save $10)*
- ❑ **Send me 2 years of digital issues for $30** (save $9.92)
- ❑ **Send me 1 year of digital issues for $17.50** (save $2.47)

Name: _____
Address: _____
City: _____ Prov. / State: _____
Postal code: _____ Country:_____
Email: _____

- ❑ Payment enclosed
- ❑ Bill me
- ❑ New
- ❑ Renewal

Make cheques payable in Canadian funds to S. Pieters. Include email address for digital editions and Paypal billing, or subscribe at www.pulpliterature.com.

*for postage outside Canada add $16 per year in North America or $32 per year overseas.